For my special Christian friend

Marilyn

Enjoy!

John Sager

# Interstate 90

## A Novel

John Sager

authorHOUSE®

AuthorHouse™
1663 Liberty Drive
Bloomington, IN 47403
www.authorhouse.com
Phone: 833-262-8899

This is a work of fiction. All of the characters, names, incidents, organizations, and dialogue
in this novel are either the products of the author's imagination or are used fictitiously.

Published by AuthorHouse 10/28/2021

ISBN: 978-1-6655-4308-8 (sc)
ISBN: 978-1-6655-4306-4 (hc)
ISBN: 978-1-6655-4307-1 (e)

Library of Congress Control Number: 2021922204

Print information available on the last page.

Any people depicted in stock imagery provided by Getty Images are models,
and such images are being used for illustrative purposes only.
Certain stock imagery © Getty Images.

This book is printed on acid-free paper.

# CONTENTS

# ONE

I T WAS STANDING ROOM ONLY FOR THE MEMORIAL SERVICE IN Mercer Island's Evergreen Covenant church. Three days earlier, Pastor Jeremy Lewis had been at Marie's bedside, holding her hand, as she quietly slipped away. She had endured a radical mastectomy five years earlier and the surgeon told her she should be fine. But, within a year, the cancer came back and this time it was fatal.

After pastor Lewis' homily, the congregation sang *How Great Thou Art*, Doris Anderson at the keyboard, she one of Marie's best friends. The mourners then moved to the back of the hall for coffee, tea and conversation. Each of them had been asked to sign the condolences book, providing a name and apartment number. It was something widower Jim Dawson would cherish for the rest of his life.

⸺⸺◆⸺⸺

Marie Dawson and her husband Jim had been among the more active residents of the Ageless Ageing retirement community on Mercer Island. She was in her mid-fifties, he five years older. Marie had been one of the leaders in the BeFrienders program and Jim often helped the community's IT technician, responding to calls for computer fixes, email Spam messages and others.

Prior to coming to their retirement community, the couple had lived in Westwood Gardens, an upscale apartment complex in Bellevue. Part of the application process for Ageless Ageing was an interview with sales manager Peter Anderson. He asked about Jim's employment history, their investments, children, health issues, any indebtedness, all of this to ensure that the couple could afford the nearly half-million dollar entry fee. All of this info goes into a computer and is password protected, they were assured. And the entry fee, although steep, eventually will go—ninety percent—to any beneficiary named in the contract.

Further into the interview, Marie had admitted that she had inherited ten million dollars from her father, one of the Seattle area's more successful real estate brokers. That money now was Jim Dawson's and he had no idea what to do with it.

He decided he should talk about this with pastor Lewis, a man he trusted and who, as a man of God, might be able to help him decide 'what's next.'

*In pastor Lewis' office:*

"Jim, if there's one thing I've learned about you it's this. You have a passion for evangelism, bringing non-believers into the Christian faith. You do it effortlessly with a smile on your face. And now, as a widower, you're probably wondering what might lie ahead."

"As usual, pastor Lewis, you're spot on. As you know by now, I'm independently wealthy, with ten million dollars burning a hole in my pocket, as the saying goes. Any ideas?"

"Your application tells us that you love to fix things, you have an above-average mechanical aptitude. Have you ever driven a truck?"

"Sure, I have my own Ford pickup truck. It's getting along, has nearly 150,000 miles and I should be looking for a trade-in. Why do you ask?"

"Okay, Jim, here's an idea for you to consider. Let's say you buy one of those eighteen wheelers, you certainly can afford to do that. I've done some online research and I've learned that Wall Mart is looking for truck drivers. The company wants to expand its operations into all forty-eight states. Let's say as a truck driver you can do 300 miles in a day, including stops along the way. If it's roughly 3,000 miles from Seattle to Boston, via Interstate 90, that's ten stops, usually overnighters. Think of the opportunities you would have during those stops. You would soon be known as the traveling evangelist, at every opportunity trying to bring people into the Christian faith."

"What about Wall Mart? Suppose they don't need another driver? And even if they did, that new driver would be competing with the other drivers and they'd probably resent that."

"Yes, you're right about that. But what you may not know is that our governor, in Olympia, is a Christian, and he and I are good friends. I can send him an email and lay out our plan and I'm sure that within hours he'll tell us to go ahead."

------◆------

After making a few phone calls, Jim decided to make the short drive to an outfit called Peterbilt Trucks of Seattle. He told the manager he was shopping for an eighteen-wheeler and, as advertised, the one he wanted was priced at $78,000. The inspection took about thirty minutes, and when he was satisfied he wrote a check for that amount and told the manager he'd come by the next day to take delivery.

But wait. Where to park this behemoth? The manager told Jim he could park/store the vehicle on the Peterbilt lot, ten dollars a day. And he could leave his Ford pickup in another lot reserved for the company's customers.

# TWO

I F HE WAS NERVOUS, HE DIDN'T SHOW IT. HE STRUGGLED UP INTO the driver's seat, fastened the seat belt and ever so slowly moved his eighteen wheeler out of the Peterbilt lot. Interstate 90 was five blocks away, down South Jackson street, with a 25 mph speed limit. Rather than use a Garmin GPS unit, Jim had decided to use his iPhone. Tap in the address of the next stop and a peasant female voice guides you to your destination.

First stop, Indian John Hill Rest Area, at mile post 89. At the trucker's speed limit of 60 mph, a few minutes under two hours. He found the men's restroom, relieved himself, bought a 50 cents cup of Starbucks and was on his way again.

Next stop, the Broadway Flying J Travel Plaza, a few miles outside of Spokane. A busy place but there's a small Seven-Eleven convenience store just inside. Jim walks in and looks for the oversized fridge, sees a six pack of Coca Cola takes it to the cashier. While she's ringing him up and pointing to the credit card machine, he sees her name tag, Francisca, probably newly-arrived from Mexico. It's a long shot, but - - -

"Hi, Francisca. How do you like working here?"

"Nice of you to ask but I don't like working here. I'm only 23 and my boss is a big flirt, thinks if he tries long enough I'll go to bed with him. But it'll never happen. I already have a six month old daughter and she's sick, doctor says it's childhood syphilis, whatever that means."

"Gee, Francisca, that's terrible!"

"Yeah, it is but that's not the whole story. I don't have a husband, one of those one night stands, as you say in English. The father is long gone and I don't even know his name."

"Have you been to a doctor? The Sacred Heart Children's hospital isn't that far from here."

"No, I can't afford to leave my job and the taxi fare to that hospital is just too

much."

"Okay, Francisca, here's what we can do. You write a note for your boss and tell him you need a couple hours time off, that it's important. I'll park my truck over there where it's out of the way. I'll call a cab, we'll pick up your daughter and we'll stop at the hospital's emergency reception area."

"Gee, that's really kind of you. What's your name?"

"It's Jim Dawson, and I'm a Christian. If you know anything about your Bible, you'll recall that Jesus wants His followers to visit the prisoners and to care for the sick. And that's what I'm doing, trying to see that your daughter is well taken care of."

———◆———

The two were ushered through the emergency waiting room, up to floor five, where Dr. Morice Franklin, the hospital's leading OBGYN, was waiting. Dr. Franklin examined infant Maria, prescribed a treatment regimen and assured the mother that her child would be well again, in six months. Jim and Francisca exchanged addresses and promised to stay in touch.

# THREE

SOON AFTER CROSSING THE IDAHO STATE LINE, JIM FOUND A truckers' rest area near Lake Coeur d' Alene and decided to spend the night there. Like nearly all eighteen wheelers, this one had a bunk bed behind the driver's seat. And it was Interstate 90's only rest stop prior to his reaching Missoula, Montana. He was too tired for an evening snack and after silently reciting Psalm 23 he fell asleep about eight p.m.

An early riser, Jim was up and dressed by six a.m., only moments after the rest area's coffee and donut shop opened for business. He filled his thermos and pocketed something like an Egg McMuffin and two Snickers bars. He was on his way twenty minutes later.

His iPhone told him he should arrive in Missoula in about two and half hours, even though the long haul up and over Lolo Pass—more than a mile above sea level—would reduce his speed to something like 25-30 mph. At the top of the pass, as he expected, there were four lanes on both sides of I-90 for truckers to pull over, use the restrooms and let their engines cool.

The ride *down* I-90 was spectacular, a few snow-capped peaks to left and right, the Bitterroot Range stretching from horizon to horizon. Jim figured he could reach the Flying J Travel Plaza in another hour, an I-90 fixture welcomed by travelers going both west and east. The Flying J was almost a community in itself: two restaurants, a coffee shop, four rest rooms, and a convenience store selling everything from bicycles to boxed lunches. And of course both diesel and gasoline pumps.

After refueling his rig, Jim pulled over to one side of the Flying J apron, shut down the engine, and headed for the convenience store. Almost immediately, he saw a slouched figure, an elderly man squatting on his haunches and mumbling to himself. He asked a nearby customer, Who is this guy?

"Oh, that's Sam Dawkins; he's a Vietnam vet, likes to come here and chat up the customers. I think Sam's in his mid-eighties, he's a widower, his wife died ten years ago and he's still mourning. They take care of him at St. Peter's Charity hospital but he gets bored there and if he's lucky he'll thumb a ride and come over here to watch the world go by."

"Is he okay, mentally?"

"No. He's slightly demented, sometime stutters, but I've never heard him say an unkind word about anybody. Fortunately, he's on Medicaid so he doesn't have to pay for anything. If you get a chance to talk to Sam he'll tell you about the good old days when he played shortstop—class A baseball, a team then known as the Missoula Marauders. But that's ancient history, although I'm not sure Sam remembers this."

•————•————•

Jim walks back into the Flying J lounge area, finds the Yellow Pages and quicky finds what he's looking for: an apartment complex about two miles to the east, *The Missoula Manor,* a facility supported by the Veterans' Administration, and intended for use by homeless and/or indigent veterans. There are fifteen one-bedroom units going for 300 dollars a month, three meals a day, laundry and a basement recreation room.

Jim walks over to the man and introduces himself.

"Hi, there Sam. How're you doing?"

"Uh, not so good. Who are you?"

"I'm Jim Dawson and I already know a little about you."

"So?"

"For one, I'm real sorry about your wife; I understand she died about ten years ago."

"Yeah, I prayed real hard that God wouldn't take her, but it didn't do no good."

"So, you're a Christian?"

"I was. Now I'm not so sure."

"You have a Bible?"

"Sure do, and I read it now and then."

"Then you know a few things about Jesus?"

"Yep."

"Do you know where He asks His followers to feed the prisoners and help heal the sick?"

"I do."

"Okay, Sam. Here's what you need to know. I'm a Christian, just like you. Have you heard of a place called Missoula Manor?"

"Can't say that I have."

"Well, it's an apartment building, not too far from here. It's supported by Missoula's Catholic church and it's reserved for people like you who don't have much money. If you're willing, I can find an apartment in that building, and it will be yours, free and clear."

"Sounds expensive and I ain't got no money."

"Don't worry about that, Sam. I've got plenty of money, much more than I need. Tell you what, let's run down there in a taxi. I'll get you checked in and you can stay there as long as you like. Comes with three meals a day, a do-it-yourself laundry and a rec room in the basement.

"And one more thing, Sam. I'll be coming back through Missoula in another month or so and I'll drop by to see how you're doing."

# FOUR

AFTER SPENDING THE NIGHT IN HIS TRUCK'S BUNK-BED, JIM KNOWS it's time to hit the road again. His next stop will be at Billings, Montana, likely a one-day drive. But to get there he has to cross over the continental divide at Homestake Pass, elevation 6,300 feet, an altitude gain of 3,100 feet. Along the way he passes by Butte, Montana, know locally as the town that's a mile high and a mile deep. Years ago, Butte produced more copper ore than anyone, and a few of the wealthy mine owner were known as The Copper Kings of the world. But, no more. Butte's current claim to fame is its home for the Montana School of Mines and Engineering.

It's a long, slow downhill run to Billings and Jim can feel his ears pop as he descends some 3,000 feet before reaching the Flying A Service Area, a few miles west of the city. He pulls into the service, parks his rig off to one side and out of the way, dismounts from the cab and walks toward two uniformed police officers. They're talking to a young woman and he can hear that her name is Donna Waite. She's telling the officers that about an hour ago she stepped up to the Seven-Eleven counter to purchase a small gift for a Christian friend and she no sooner pockets the change than this guy appears from nowhere, whispers that he has a knife and she'd better do what he says. She and he back peddle into the truckers' lounge. He locks the door and forces her onto one of the couches and with his knife at her throat tells her she needs to

10

remove her slacks and panties or die. She struggles free just long enough to scream and unlock the door. Moments later the police offers have the guy in handcuffs. They demand to see his wallet then check his name via their car radio.

Sure enough. His name is John Valko and there's a year-old outstanding warrant for his arrest for attempted rape.

One of the officers tells his partner he wants to offer Mr. Valko a kind of plea-bargain. Valko will be let go if he confesses to the attempted rape but there will be a record of this event in the Billings' police files. And if it happens again, he'll be arrested, imprisoned and tried by a judge and jury.

# FIVE

JIM WAS IN NO HURRY TO GET GOING. GILLETTE, WYOMING WAS NO more than a three hour drive and he could be there in time for lunch. Before getting underway, he'd done a bit of research with his laptop computer. Somewhat to his surprise, he learned that Gillette and the surrounding area provide 35 percent of the nation's coal, through a process known as surface coal mining. The area is also rich in natural gas and the areas' citizens think of themselves as the Energy Capital of America.

The city lies on a high plateau, nearly a mile above sea level, with a population of about 33,000 people. About a third of them are in some way linked to coal production and according to the most recent census, the average family income is about $80,000. Aside from its reputation as an area rich in energy resources, Gillette is home to the U.S. Army's High Mobility Artillery Rocket system.

According to the Wikipedia account he found on his laptop, in recent years, soldiers from the 2nd Battalion, 300th Field Artillery have been deployed in Iraq for something called Operation Enduring Freedom. The Iraq war lasted for eight years, and this weapon played a large role. The projectile is a guided missile with a range of about 185 miles. The weapon also has seen service in Afghanistan and Syria.

'Interesting info,' Jim says to himself. But I'm pooped.

---

For a change, Jim decides to spend the night in Gillette. He pulls his rig off to one side of the Flying J tarmac, receives permission to leave it there overnight. Then he hails a cab and asks to be taken to the Radisson Hotel. After checking in, he goes to his room on the second floor, showers, shaves, changes clothes and takes a much-needed two-hour nap.

It's now time for an early dinner. Jim walks into a nearly-empty dining room asks the maître d to assign him a table.

"Any table you like, Sir. There's a young man over there; you might care to join him. He's well known in these parts, works with the Army's High Mobility Artillery Rocket system. Staff Sergeant Billy McKay is his name, he served in Iraq."

"Thanks, Garcia, I'll do that."

---

"Mind if I join you? The maître d gave me your name. Said you've served in Iraq. I've never been a military man myself, but I admire those who have."

"Sure, have seat. I'm Billy McKay and you are- -"

"Jim Dawson. I drive a truck for Wall Mart, just passing through. I'm curious to know more about your service, if you're willing to share."

"Yeah, I have a story you should be interested in and you can take it with you and share it with others."

"How so?"

"I have a buddy. We did time together in Iraq. You don't need to know his name but you should know what he's up to. He's pissed off about this guided missile rig we're working on. Says it's a real threat to world peace. And I swear this is true; he wants to sabotage the thing, make it inoperable so the Army will decide to scrap it."

"Have you reported this to the authorities?"

"No. If the Army finds out I could be court-marshalled."

"What if I were to report it, without naming you or anyone else?"

"That's okay with me. But why would you want to do that?

"Okay, Billy. You need to know that I'm a Christian. I'm one of Jesus' many followers. If you've read your Bible lately, you'll know that Jesus was a man of peace. And by blowing the whistle on this crazy plot, we'll all be a tiny bit closer to that peace."

———◆———

Jim immediately seeks an audience with Gillette's National Guard captain, Jack Nelson, himself an Iraq veteran. After hearing the story, Nelson sends an email to Colonel Robert Samson, the officer in charge of all Wyoming's U.S. Army operations. Within one week, the High Mobility Artillery Rocket system is put on hold. The next day a reporter for the Gillette *News Record* asked Colonel Samson for an explanation. He was told the matter was highly classified and he had no further comment.

———◆———

After a good Saturday night's sleep, Jim has breakfast in the hotel's dining room. Then, at ten the next morning he takes a cab to the *Living Life* church and after hearing the pastor's sermon he hands one of the ushers a note in which he promises to come again, on his way back along Interstate 90.

# SIX

Next stop, Rapid City, South Dakota. Jim's laptop computer gave him a brief introduction to the city:

'Rapid City's economy is diverse, but industry is a small portion, as is typical of many US cities in the 21st century. Heavy and medium industrial activities include a Portland Cement plant (constructed and owned for 84 years by the State of South Dakota and sold in 2003 to Grupo Cementos de Chihuahua, or GCC, a Mexican-based conglomerate); Black Hills Ammunition, an ammunition and reloading supplies manufacturing company; several custom sawmills, a lime plant, a computer peripheral component manufacturing plant, and several farm and ranch equipment manufacturers. Of particular note, the city is the center for the manufacture of Black Hills gold jewelry a popular product with tourists and Westerners in general. The city is the site of the only American manufacturer of stamping machines used for the labeling of plywood and chipboard products.'

He knew his next layover would be in the large parking lot, servicing visitors to the Mt. Rushmore Memorial, near Rapid City, South Dakota. Jim had read about the Memorial and seen pictures of it but he thought it about time that he took a few pictures for his own collection. It was about ten in the morning and the lot was already packed with tourists.

Jim could see a number of RVs and 18 wheelers parked off to one side so he found an empty space, lowered himself from the cab, locked it and walked over to a nearby bench, camera in hand with a telephoto lens attached.

After the third exposure, he looked back to see what he'd done; 'Looks good, he said to himself.'

He looked up to see a young woman walking toward him. She smiled and asked Jim if she could join him. She was quite pretty, about five/five, wearing sun glasses, slacks and a souvenir blouse stenciled 'I've seen Mt. Rushmore.'

Her name, Suzzanne Jamison, a high school senior at Rapid City high school. She tells Jim that her teacher has asked her and her classmates to find an 'interesting person,' interview him/her and write a human-interest story for the school's weekly newspaper. She tells Jim that she saw him leave an 18-wheeler and she assumes he's a truck driver. Truck drivers must live interesting lives, she says, and would Jim agree to an interview?

Of course he would, but where? Sitting on this bench won't work. Suzzanne has the answer. We'll go to my parents' home and have lunch there.

------◆------

It had been weeks since Jim was able to enjoy a home-cooked meal and this one was very good: chilled tomato aspic, split pea soup with oyster crackers, pieces of home-made flat bread and iced tea.

After lunch, Mrs. Jamison excused herself and the three retired to the home's living room. Suzzanne's father, Peter Jamison, told Jim that he's employed full time at Mt. Rushmore, as a National Park Service Ranger. And, recently, his job is beginning to be more challenging.

Everybody knows how social media affects the behavior of teenagers. Only yesterday, for example, a kid about seventeen drove up in a battered station wagon, leaving two of his buddies watch while he lit up a joint. When he was nearly falling-down stupefied, he staggered off to one side of the parking area, pulled down his pants, relieved himself and returned to his friends. They began hooping and hollering, as though it was the funniest thing they'd ever seen.

Even worse, two days ago, about quitting time, a teen arrived with his girlfriend. They appeared to be intoxicated and headed for the ladies' restroom. Within a few minutes she was giggling and sighing loud enough to be heard and it was obvious that they were having sex. A few minutes later a male voice, 'let's do it again, soon.' She: 'Don't forget your condom!'

---

Jim wants to know where these kids go to school. Jamison says they're all students at Rapid City high school. What's the school's principal say about this? He's talked to him many times but he says there's nothing he can do about it. The parents don't complain, probably because they don't know what their kids are doing.

Jim: What about church? Are any of these kids Christians?

Jamison: Yes, two of them are and I know their parents. Matter of fact they're members of our local Young Life chapter. When they go— not very often—they attend a small Baptist church, about ten miles east of here. The pastor's name is Wayne Hansen, ordained three years ago, so he's fairly new."

Jim: What if we were to talk to him? Maybe he'd be willing to help, after he hears our story.

---

An hour later, in Hansen's office, the young pastor welcomed his two visitors and it soon became apparent why they were there. He reminded them that only two days ago, at seven in the evening, he had supervised a Young Life gathering. It had been attended by four of the high school's leadership team, all four seniors, two boys and two girls. One of the girls, Marsha Hamilton, was aware of the sexual encounter in the women's restroom at the Mt. Rushmore parking lot. The girl—her name is Nancy Gardner—is a fiend of hers and has admitted that she fears she may be pregnant. The boy, Billy Norris, is one of the school's well-known trouble makers. The school's principal has threatened to have him expelled, not once, but twice.

Jim suggests that pastor Hansen invite both Nancy and Billy to his office, tell the two of them that he's aware of their sexual relationship and remind them that they are, after all, two Christians. Is this the kind of behavior that Jesus would approve? Of course not.

———————◆———————

And that is what happened. Billy and Nancy met with pastor Hansen once a week for six weeks, Thursday evenings from seven to eight. They prayed, hummed spiritual songs, and promised God to do their best to live as Jesus would want them to.

Jim—on the road again—received an email from the pastor in which he reported the good news. He sent a return message, promising to visit Rapid City on his way back, along Interstate 90.

# SEVEN

E VER CURIOUS, AND KNOWING THAT SIOUX FALLS, SOUTH DAKOTA, would be his next layover, Jim again went to his laptop, called up Wikipedia and saw before him, he thought, more than he wanted to know.

◆ ┅┅◆┅┅ ◆

'The history of Sioux Falls revolves around the cascades of the Big Sioux River. The falls were created about 14,000 years ago during the last ice age. The lure of the falls has been a powerful influence. Ho-Chunk, Ioway, Otoe, Missouri, Omaha (and Ponca at the time), Quapaw, Kansa, Osage, Arikira, Dakota, and Cheyenne people inhabited and settled the region previous to Europeans and European descendants. Several burial mounds still exist on the high bluffs near the river and are spread throughout the general vicinity. Indigenous people maintained an agricultural society with fortified villages, and the later arrivals rebuilt on many of the same sites that were previously settled. The Lakota Native Americans populate urban and reservation communities in the contemporary state and many Lakota, Dakota, and numerous other Indigenous Americans reside in Sioux Falls today.

'French voyagers/explorers visited the area in the early 18th century. The first documented visit by an American of European descent was by Philander Prescott who camped overnight at the falls in December

19

1832. Captain James Allen led a military expedition out of Fort Des Moines in 1844. Jacob Ferris described the Falls in his 1856 book "The States and Territories of the Great West".

'Two separate groups, the Dakota Land Company of St. Paul and the Western Town Company of Dubuque, Iowa organized in 1856 to claim the land around the falls, considered a promising townsite for its beauty and water power. Each laid out 320-acre claims, but worked together for mutual protection. They built a temporary barricade of turf which they dubbed "Fort Sod", in response to native tribes attempting to defend their land from the settlers. Seventeen men then spent "the first winter" in Sioux Falls. The following year the population grew to near 40.

'Although conflicts in Minnehaha County between Native American and white settlers were few, the Dakota War of 1862 engulfed nearby southwestern Minnesota. The town was evacuated in August of that year when two local settlers were killed as a result of the conflict. The settlers and soldiers stationed there traveled to Yankton in late August 1862. The abandoned townsite was pillaged and burned.

'Fort Dakota, a military reservation established in present-day downtown, was established in May 1865. Many former settlers gradually returned and a new wave of settlers arrived in the following years. The population grew to 593 by 1873, and a building boom was underway in that year. The Village of Sioux Falls, consisting of 1,200 acres, was incorporated in 1876 and was granted a city charter by the Dakota Territorial legislature on March 3, 1883.

'The arrival of the railroads ushered in the great Dakota Boom decade of the 1880s. The population of Sioux Falls mushroomed from 2,164 in 1880 to 10,167 at the close of the decade. The growth transformed the city. A severe plague of grasshoppers and a national depression halted the boom by the early 1890s. The city grew by only 89 people from 1890 to 1900.

'But prosperity eventually returned with the opening of the John Morrell meat packing plant in 1909, the establishment of an airbase and a military radio and communications training school in 1942, and the completion of the interstate highways in the early 1960s. Much of the growth in the first part of the 20th century was fueled by agriculturally based industry, such as the Morrell plant and the nearby stockyards, one of the largest in the nation.

'In 1955 the city decided to consolidate the neighboring incorporated city of South Sioux Falls. At the time South Sioux Falls had a population of nearly 1,600 inhabitants, according to the 1950 census. It was the third largest city in the county after Sioux Falls and Dell Rapids. By October 18, 1955, South Sioux Falls residents voted 704 in favor and 227 against to consolidate with Sioux Falls. On the same issue, Sioux Falls residents voted on November 15 by the vote 2,714 in favor and 450 against.

'In 1981, to take advantage of recently relaxed state usury laws, Citibank relocated its primary credit card center from New York City to Sioux Falls. Some claim that this event was the primary impetus for the increased population and job growth rates that Sioux Falls has experienced over the past quarter-century. Others point out that Citibank's relocation was only part of a more general transformation of the city's economy from an industrially based one to an economy centered on health care, finance, and retail trade.

'Sioux Falls has grown at a rapid pace since the late 1970s, with the city's population increasing from 81,000 in 1980 to 195,850 in 2020.

---

'On the night of September 10, 2019, the south side of Sioux Falls was hit by three EF-2 three EF2 tornadoes, severely damaging at least 37 buildings, including the Plaza 41 Shopping Center. One tornado hit the Avera Heart Hospital, damaging portions of the roof and windows, and causing 7 injuries, including a man who fractured his skull as he was thrown into an exterior wall of the hospital. Another tornado hit the busy commercial district near the Empire Mall, injuring one woman inside her home. Another touched down on the far south side in a suburban residential area, tearing the roofs off homes. The total damage was more than $5 million.

'Sioux Falls has more than 70 parks and greenways. Probably the best known is Falls Park, established around the city's namesake waterfalls on the Big Sioux River, just north of downtown. Other notable parks include Terrace Park, McKennan Park, Sherman Park, and Yankton Trail park. A popular feature of the park system is a paved 19-mile path used for biking, jogging, and walking. The path follows the course of the Big Sioux River, forming a loop around Sioux Falls, along with a few spurs off the main bike trail. Recently the city stepped up efforts to beautify a stretch of the bike trails through downtown along an area known as the River Greenway. Two of three planned phases of construction and updates have occurred. Among the updates were newer widened bike paths, new landscaping and lighting, improved street access to the bike trails, a new interactive fountain, a new pedestrian bridge across the river, removal of the old "River Ramp" parking structure, new stepped terraces leading down to the river's edge, new retaining walls along portions of the river, and a new amphitheater/performing space. New trailheads at Elmen, Dunham, and Lien parks have helped to improve access to outlying trail spurs. The city is expanding the bike trail network east from Sioux Falls at Lien Park to Brandon, South Dakota, and ultimately the Big Sioux Recreation Area. The South Dakota Department of Game, Fish and Parks has an outdoor campus in Sioux Falls at Sertoma Park with several outdoor areas and acreages devoted to fish and wildlife. The outdoor campus Great Bear Recreation Park hosts many outdoor activities, including stargazing and snowshoeing. During the winter, if offers skiing, snowboarding, and tubing.

———◆———

'Due to its inland location, Sioux Falls experiences a humid Continental climate, characterize by hot, humid summers and cold, dry winters. The monthly daily average temperature ranges from 16.6 °F in January to 73.0 °F in July; there are 18 days of maxima at or above 90 °F and 26 days with minima at or below 0 °F annually. Snowfall occurs mostly in light to moderate amounts during the winter, totaling 44.6 inches. Precipitation, at 26.33 inches annually, is concentrated in the warmer months. This results in frequent thunderstorms in summer from convection being built up with the unstable weather patterns. Extremes range from –42 °F on February 9, 1899 to 110 °F as recently as June 21, 1988.'

———◆———

His iPhone told him the nearest rest area was called Valley Springs and, sure enough, it was like many—huge, with rest rooms, a snack bar, and plenty of room for his eighteen wheeler. Jim dismounted, walked directly to the men's room, relieved himself, grabbed a cup of coffee and plopped down on a nearby bench. It was approaching noon and he thought he should grab a bite to eat, but not here. Then he sees someone, a man about his age, and asks him if he can recommend a good restaurant.

"Sure I can. I guess you don't want to eat here, right?"

"Well, I could, but I've been on the road long enough that a decent meal would help."

"Okay, if you have the time you can ride into the city with me. My car's parked right over there and it's no more than a ten minutes drive."

⸺⸺⸺◆⸺⸺⸺

The 'car' turns out to be a 2020 Mercedes convertible but its owner, Dan Thomas, prefers to drive with the top down. It's quieter that way and easier to talk. Thomas identifies himself as a member of the Sioux Falls city council, he's a Republican and a Christian.

Over lunch—a cheeseburger, fries and root beer—Thomas talks about his problems as a member of the city's ten-person council. For one, the mayor is a liberal Democrat and he intends to impose a four cents a gallon tax on all purchases of gasoline and diesel fuel, claiming this will be the city's contribution to the fight against global warming. Worse, probably, at the next city-wide election—two months away—the mayor will put on the ballot a proposal for adding a three cents a gallon tax on every vehicle owned by the city. And on the same ballot will be a recommendation for adding a three cents a pound tax for every product coming out of the John Morrell meat packing plant, the city's largest source of taxable income.

⸺⸺⸺◆⸺⸺⸺

"What can we do to stop this?"

"Jim, it's a long shot but I have an idea that might work. We know that this city and state are pretty conservative, have been for ages. Of course, our mayor knows this, too. Here's what he's planning to do, in fact his idea may already be gaining traction. He has asked each one of us council members to connect with every church in the city and try to persuade the pastors, or other church leaders, to support his tax proposals. I'm having nothing to do with this, but I can only speak for myself. It's the others I'm worried about."

"In addition to yourself, how many?"

"Nine, and I'm on pretty good terms with each one of them."

"Look, Dan, I'm prepared to stay here for as long as it takes. Let's say you arrange a private get-together with each council member, one each evening in the person's home. The two of us explain the folly of the mayor's proposals. Those council members who are Christians will be even more impressed by what we have to say. Our best appeal is to remind each of them that the very early settlers in this country insisted that there could be no taxation without representation. That is exactly what's happening here."

———◆———

Two weeks later the Sioux Falls leading TV outlet, ABC's KFSY, reported that liberal mayor Dennis Gray had tendered his resignation, subject to approval by the city's council. At the same time, three of the council's liberal members also resigned.

Councilman Dan Thomas, responding to a reporter's question, said it was all in a day's work. He had help from the driver of one of Wall Mart's eighteen wheelers, who asked that his name not be revealed.

# EIGHT

Jim's next layover, as he had planned it, would be Madison, Wisconsin, about 450 miles distant and a nine-hour drive. He didn't like pushing it that hard, nine hours without a break, so he stopped at an I-90 rest area, took an hour's nap, and was on his way again.

About thirty minutes west of the Madison city limits, Jim spotted a large rest area, plenty of room for his eighteen-wheeler. He was still tired so he hailed a cab and asked the driver to take him to one of the finer Madison hotels.

"You can't beat the Hilton Madison Monona Terrace, if you're willing to pay two hundred bucks a night"

"That's okay, take me there. I'm pooped and could use a decent meal after a hot shower and shave."

———◆———

Jim quickly sees that the hotel has a very nice dining room, so he decides to order dinner before going up to his room for the night. Before being shown his table, he asks the head waiter if he's likely to meet any of Madison's leading citizens, given the cost of staying in such an expensive hotel.

"Sure, right over there. That's doctor Gerald Smithson, the head of Wisconsin's dairy certification board. He has a lot of influence around here."

———◆———

The doctor turns out to be a personable man, easy to talk to and very much interested in Jim's travel—all the way to Boston! Jim tells him he wants to pay for lunch. And, by the way, back home he buys cheese from Wisconsin, especially Wisconsin Blue Vein cheese. It's really identical to the French Roquefort, but the French have an international patent on that name.

But that's not what Jim has in mind. He wants to know what the good doctor does for a living.

"Jim, I'm paid employee of the state of Wisconsin. I'm in charge of the state's Dairy Certification Board. That means that every rancher in this state who raises cows for milk production has to meet our approval. We issue licenses, once a year, and our inspectors are constantly going from one dairy to another, making sure they're in compliance with our rules."

"What kind of rules?"

"Okay. The pasteurizing process goes like this. The chilled, raw milk is heated by passing between heated stainless steel plates until the milk reaches 161°F. It stays at this temperature for at least 15 seconds to kill bacteria before it is quickly cooled back to its original temperature of 39 degrees."

"But, you've implied that you're having trouble enforcing your rules."

"That's right. Some of the ranchers are selling milk that hasn't been properly processed; usually, they skimp on the heating process and this fails to kill the microbes that bring on E. coli, Listeria and Salmonella. I believe they're motivated by the fact that the profit margin on milk sales is very small. Still, that's no excuse for breaking the rules."

"What can you do about it?"

"Not much. These ranchers are all part of the local union—a subset of the AFL/CIO—and it's nearly impossible to bring legal action against them."

"Hmm. Are any of the local churches aware of this?"

"Some are. Why do you ask?"

"Let's say we persuade one of the local churches to file a law suit against the union. Which church has the most influence in these parts?"

"No doubt it's the Luther Memorial church. They're part of the ELCA, the Evangelical Lutheran Church of America. A good friend mine is a member of that church and he's told me that serval attorneys attend worship services."

"What do you think it would cost to hire one of these attorneys and he files a lawsuit against the union?"

"Hard to say. I'd guess at least five, six thousand, maybe as much as ten."

"Doctor Smithson, I haven't mentioned this yet but you should know that I'm a Christian. I consider myself a kind of traveling evangelist. I also happen to be quite wealthy. When my wife died some time ago she left me a multi-millionaire. So, paying for this lawsuit won't hurt me a bit."

---

The lawsuit proceeded with unusual speed. When the depositions were studied, it was clear that the union was a fault and its leader decided to enter a plea of guilty, providing the news media remain unaware. After a thirty minute meeting in the office of the union's chief negotiator, he gave his word that the union's members would change their ways and welcome the health inspectors at any time.

# NINE

Her name is Marie Dubois, a fourth generation French-American whose grandparents were among the first to move to the Pacific Northwest. At age 22, Marie made a name for herself by modeling the latest women's fashions for the now-defunct Bon Marché, then Seattle's go-to purveyor of women's clothing. At the time she was considered one of Seattle's most beautiful women and talented. She could sing, she could dance and she was an accomplished pianist.

Unfortunately, Marie has outlived three husbands and, at age 84, she now resides at the Ageless Aging retirement community on Mercer Island, Washington. Her granddaughter, Susan Dubois, has inherited most of her grandmother's wealth and lives in the Hunt's Point gated community, at one time the residence of Bill and Melinda Gates.

---

At a recent worship service, pastor Jeremy Lewis recognized Marie, noting that after many years' residence in the facility she was about to move to other quarters. Soon after the service ended, Marie phoned her granddaughter Susan with the good news.

This set Susan to thinking. She's heard compelling stories from her grandmother about Jim Dawson, the wealthy truck driver who runs an eighteen wheeler for Wall Mart. She knows Jim is single and, from what she's heard, he's a committed Christian who likes to spread the Gospel wherever possible. How to connect with Jim? Ask her grandmother to get Jim's schedule from Chaplain Lewis. Surely they're in touch with each other.

The very next day Susan sends an email to Jim Dawson, introducing herself and saying she'd like very much to meet him, that she's writing human interest stories for *The Seattle Times* and she imagines she could write a story about how a Pacific Northwest resident is making a name for himself.

---

Surprised, for sure. But Jim's curiosity gets the best of him and he responds to Susan's email. He's booked into Chicago's Palmer House Hilton hotel where he intends to spend the next two-three days. And, yes, she's welcome to find him there.

Next, Jim uses his iPhone and after two false starts he's connected to the *Seattle Times* assistant editor.

"Who? Susan Dubois? No, never heard of her. Why do you ask?"

"It's nothing, I was only curious. Sorry to bother you."

"Hmm, as they say the thought plickens. So Susan wants to play games, does she? Well, I'll be more than happy to help her do that."

---

With Jim's 'green light' in hand, Susan is able to book a flight on Delta Airlines, first class, round trip for a little less that a thousand dollars. After negotiating the zoo at Chicago's O'Hare airport, she hails a cab and asks to be taken to the city's Palmer House Hilton hotel. While waiting in the arrivals terminal, she phones the hotel and, yes, there are a few available rooms, $250 a night for a single bed, breakfast included.

"Would you please ring Mr. James Dawson for me?"

"Sorry, Miss, Mr. Dawson isn't here right now. Perhaps you can call later."

◆

Susan hails a cab and asks to be taken to the hotel. She checks in, using her American Express credit card, and tells the clerk that Mr. Dawson is a friend of hers and could she have a room on the same floor?

The clerk obliges, tells her that room 1542 is across the hall from his. And the view from the fifteenth floor is spectacular.

Susan tips the bellboy with a twenty dollar bill, closes the door and tosses her overnight bag on the bed. She changes clothes, puts on her 'come get me' outfit—with a tiny splash of Tiffany—and walks across the hall to room 1543 and pushes the door bell.

To her surprise the door opens and there stands Jim Dawson, all smiles.

"Well, helo there! And who might you be?"

"I'm Susan Dubois. I've come all the way from Seattle to find you and here I am, at last!"

"Why me?"

"Well, it's because I write human interest stories for the Seattle Times newspaper. I've done some research and I think you'd be a great candidate for an interview, what with all the traveling you've been doing."

"You're too pretty to be working for a newspaper."

"Thank you, Mr. Dawson. Yes, most me do find me attractive, an accident of birth, you could call it."

"Speaking of which, where were you born?"

"In Seattle. I love it there, in spite of the rain."

"How long do you plan to be in Chicago?"

31

"As long as it takes, probably not more than two-three days."

"Are you alone or with someone?"

"Nope, I'm all by myself. I have a room close by."

"What say we have lunch together? I've seen the menu and it's superb."

⸻ ◆ ⸻

Following lunch, Jim tells Susan that he's quite tired, didn't get much sleep last night and he'd like to take a nap. Thirty minutes, no more. Back in his room, he flops down on the bed, shoes off, and begins to think about what's happening. Obviously this pretty young thing is no more a writer than the downstairs desk clerk. She must have plenty of money to have flown here just to see me. She's staying in one of the most expensive rooms in this hotel, so what's her game? Maybe she's looking for a husband, I didn't see a ring on her left hand. Or maybe she wants sex and if that's the case, then she's barking up the wrong tree. Best I be nice to her and we'll see where this goes. She's never been in the Willis Tower, nor have I. So that's what we'll do. We'll have dinner in that restaurant at the bottom of the tower, then go up to the Skydeck and we'll see if she's willing to step out onto The Ledge. It's what, more than a thousand feet above the sidewalk, and most people get dizzy, or worse, when they do that.

⸻ ◆ ⸻

Jim pulled out his laptop, brought up Wikipedia and read about the Willis Tower.

'The Willis Tower (formerly known as and commonly referred to as the Sears Tower) is a 108 story, 1,450-foot skyscraper in Chicago. The tower has 108 stories as counted by standard methods, though the building's owners count the main roof as 109 and the mechanical penthouse roof as 110. At completion in 1974, it surpassed the World Trade Center in New York City to become the tallest building in the world, a title that it held for nearly 25 years; it was also the tallest building in the Western Hemisphere for 41 years, until the new One World Trade Center surpassed it 2013.

'Willis Tower is considered a seminal achievement for engineer Fazlur Rahman Khan. It is currently the third-tallest building in the United States and the Western Hemisphere—and the 23$^{rd}$ tallest in the world. Each year, more than one million people visit its observation deck, the highest in the United States, making it one of Chicago's most popular tourist destinations. The structure was renamed in 2009 by the Willis Group, as a term of its lease.

'As of April 2018, the building's largest tenant is United Airlines, which moved its corporate headquarters from the United Building in 2012, occupying some 20 floors. Other major tenants include the building's namesake Willis Towers Watson and the law firms Schiff, Hardin and Seyfarth Shah. Morgan Stanley plans to move into the building soon and will become its fourth-largest tenant by 2020.

'It was named the Sears Tower until 2009, serving as the headquarters of retail company Sears, Roebuck from its opening in 1974 to 1994. However, local area residents still refer to the building by its old name.'

***

Jim assumed that his date had a lot more money than he'd ever see, but it was his treat. Susan was wearing something that remined him of one of those beautiful New York fashion models, revealing what mattered but no more than that.

They took a cab from the hotel to the ground floor of the Willis Tower, walked through the revolving doors and were met by the hotel's concierge.

He told them their table was ready, in one of the tower's three restaurants. They can find it on the tenth floor, the *Golden Steer Steak House.*

———◆———

"Okay, Susan, this is my treat so order whatever you like. There's a separate list of available wines, and we can choose from that as soon as we decide on the main course."

"That's very generous of you, Jim. I'd like to try the rib steak entrée, along with asparagus tips in sauce Bearnaise, sautéed mushrooms and chilled chopped carrots."

"Sounds good. Just to make things simple for the kitchen, I'll order the same.

"Wine?"

"Yes, I believe we can share a bottle. I see a 2009 Chilean Malbec. Would that be okay with you?"

"Of course. Anything you say."

———◆———

They ate in near silence, occasionally mentioning how well-prepared everything was. For dessert, Susan suggested Tiramisu, and decaf coffee.

As soon as the waiter cleared their table, the couple moved onto the restaurant's tiny dance floor. The five piece orchestra was playing *When Smoke Gets In Your Eyes,* soft, slow, melodic. Jim was aware that Susan was holding him as close as the law allowed and he began to feel that danger sign between his thighs. 'Slow down, Jim, this could be trouble.'

———◆———

"Where did you learn to dance, Jim? You're very good at it."

"Thanks, Susan. My mom insisted that I learn. She was pretty insistent about my learning the 'social graces,' as she put it. Problem is, with my job I have very few opportunities to do this."

"Speaking of which, you haven't said much about your job."

"Tell you what, Susan, let's have breakfast together tomorrow morning and I'll tell you more than you want to know!"

————————◆————————

And Jim did just that. Took almost an hour but when he was finished Susan agreed that she was right. He *was* worth an interview. But, hey, she could do that while they were sightseeing. Jim had promised to take her to the top of the Willis Tower and the two of them had yet to try some of the city's famous pizza palaces. And what about shopping along the city's Magnificent Mile?

They were both hungry after an early breakfast and Jim said he knew just the place for lunch: Pedro's Pizza Palace, one of the city's best-known pizza emporiums, about two blocks from where they were standing.

Although the place was crowded, the headwaiter found a table next to a window, good for watching the hurried pedestrian traffic along the sidewalk. After scanning the menu, Jim recommended a deep-dish pizza, with pickled mushrooms, mozzarella cheese, Italian salami and diced garlic cloves, but easy on the garlic.

"What about you, Susan? The same or something different?"

"No, that's fine. But don't we want beer to go with the pizza?"

"Of course, dumb of me to forget. They have Corona from Mexico, Heineken from Holland, and the old American favorite, Pabst Blue Ribbon."

"Believe it or not, I've never tried Heineken so I'll go with that."

"Super, Susan, I'll do the same."

————————◆————————

The first beer was followed by one more and then another. As they got up to leave, Jim could see that she was a bit tipsy. He suggested she visit the lady's room and while she did that he paid the bill and hailed a taxi. The Magnificent Mile could wait but why not do the Willis Tower? That would be a new experience for each of them; Jim was pleased to learn that the ride to the top of the tower was free.

———◆———

"You sure you're ready for this, Susan? It's a long way up, nearly one-third of a mile, or one thousand four hundred and fifty feet, according to this brochure."

"Of course I'm ready, so let's go!"

The ride up was remarkably brief, no more than four minutes, according to Jim's watch. When the elevator stopped, some twenty tourists—including Jim and Susan—stepped out onto the observation deck. Jim had read about the so-called Ledge, a plexiglass 'box' large enough for four persons at a time. He took Susan by the elbow and guided her into the enclosed Ledge.

"Look, Susan, straight down you can see the sidewalk and some pedestrians. That's almost 1,500 feet."

"Yes, and It makes me dizzy. I think we should leave."

"Sure, your call."

———◆———

An hour later, back in her hotel room, Susan decided it was time to level with Jim Dawson. She knew she was falling in love with the man, something that could never lead to marriage. 'He's on the road most of the time and I've no right to ask him to give that up.'

She decided to leave him a note, slipped under his hotel room door.

*My dearest Jim. You may not be aware but I have to admit it. I have fallen in love with you, something that could never lead to marriage. I sometimes think about how wonderful it would be if we were to go to bed together, but then I know you're a Christian and that your Jesus would never approve.*

*I've decided to return to Seattle And don't worry, I can find my way to the airport.*

*I'll always love you, Jim, but I'd better go now, before I make a fool of myself.*

# TEN

Aᴄᴛᴇʀ ʀᴇᴀᴅɪɴɢ ᴛʜᴇ ɴᴏᴛᴇ, Jɪᴍ ᴅᴇᴄɪᴅᴇᴅ ᴛʜᴀᴛ ʙᴏᴛʜ ʜᴇ ᴀɴᴅ Susan had done the right thing. She by being up front and honest and he by never trying to establish a romantic relationship. A pity, though, she really is a remarkable woman.

He knew that Cleveland, Ohio was his next stop, a run of nearly six hours, and he'd better get a good night's sleep before heading out. He put in a wakeup call with the hotel's front desk, 0600. But before going to bed he pulled out his laptop to see what Wikipedia has to say about Cleveland.

⸻ ◆ ⸻

'Cleveland was founded in 1796 near the mouth of the Cuyahoga River by General Moses Cleveland, after whom the city was named. It grew into a major manufacturing center due to its location on both the river and the lake shore, as well as numerous canals and railroad lines. A port city, Cleveland is connected to the Atlantic Ocean via the Saint Lawrence Seaway. The city's economy relies on diversified sectors such as manufacturing, financial services, healthcare, biomedicals, and higher education. The gross domestic product for the Greater Cleveland area was $135 billion in 2019. Combined with the Akron region, the seven-county Cleveland–Akron metropolitan economy was $175 billion in 2019, the largest in Ohio, accounting for 25% of the state's GDP.

'The city's boundaries were defined on July 22, 1796, by surveyors of the Connecticut Land Company when they laid out the state's Western Reserve into townships and a capital city.

'The settlement served as an important supply post for the U.S. during the Battle of Lake Erie during the War of 1812. Local residents adopted Commodore Oliver Hazard Perry as a civic hero and decades later erected a monument in his honor. The Village of Cleveland was incorporated on December 23, 1814. In spite of the nearby swampy lowlands and harsh winters, the town's waterfront location proved to be an advantage, giving it access to Great Lakes trade. It grew rapidly after the 1832 completion of the Ohio and Erie Canal. This key link between the Ohio River and the Great Lakes connected it to the Atlantic Ocean via the Erie Canal and Hudson River, and later via the Saint Lawrence Seaway. Its products could reach markets on the Gulf of Mexico via the Mississippi River. The town's growth continued with added railroad links.

'In 1831, the spelling of the town's name was altered by *The Cleveland Advertiser* newspaper. In order to fit the name on the newspaper's masthead, the editors dropped the first "a", reducing the city's name to *Cleveland*, which eventually became the official spelling. In 1836, Cleveland, then only on the eastern banks of the Cuyahoga River, was officially incorporated as a city.

'Home to a vocal group of abolitionists, Cleveland (code-named "Station Hope") was a major stop on the Underground Railroad for escaped African-American slaves enroute to Canada. The city also served as an important center for the Union during America's Civil War.

'Decades later, in July 1894, the wartime contributions of those

39

serving the Union from Cleveland and Cuyahoga County would be honored with the opening of the city's Soldiers' and Sailors' Monument on Public Square.'

———◆———

Jim's Wikipedia search also helped him decide where to stop, as close to downtown Cleveland as possible. The Concord rest area looked to be about ten miles east of the city and that would have to do.

It was a little after ten when he pulled his rig off to one side, reached for his iPhone and called for a cab.

Ten minutes later he told the driver he wanted to be taken to the Church of the Covenant, about two miles south of the I-90 interchange, on Euclid Avenue. Jim had learned that this church was added to the National Register of Historic Places in 1980 and he wanted to see it for himself.

When he stepped out of the cab, he saw a directory at the foot of the church's steps. It told him what he was looking for, the pastor's name and address: Rev. Jeremy Whitworth, parsonage 50 yards to your left, visiting hours ten to two.

Jim punched the doorbell, it opened and there was the Reverend Jeremy Whitworth.

"Please, come in. You are - - -?"

"James, or Jim. Jim Dawson. I drive an eighteen wheeler for Wall Mart. I'm a Christian, a kind of traveling evangelist. I'm new to this area and would like to see more of it."

"Sounds interesting. Tell me more."

"My home is on Mercer Island, Washington. Soon after my wife died, a minister encouraged me to do some traveling, to spread the Gospel. He—we—decided the best way to do this was for me to hit the road, so to speak. I had enough money so I could afford to buy this eighteen wheeler and the minister arranged with Wall Mart that I would represent them as I go from place to place. But my principal purpose is try to persuade others to accept Jesus.

"And I'm here to help you, if you need help."

"Hmm, matter of fact I could use some help. You see, Jim, this church is well-known, what with that National Register recognition. And because we're well known, we have about 300 worshippers who come here every Sunday. That means we do three services; one begins at nine, the second at one and the third about five o'clock. And I have two associate pastors who help.

"But it's our youth program that worries me."

"How so?"

"Okay. Teenagers only, both boys and girls. And it's no secret that some of these kids are using drugs; mostly marijuana but now and then the harder stuff. We have a rule that prohibits anyone from coming if he/she is under the influence. Of course, these kids are smart enough to figure a way around the rules. They'll insist they're sober when they're not. To deal with this, I'll ask an offender to tell me about something he/she has read in the Bible, say John's second letter, very brief and to the point. They'll look at me as though I just fell off the turnip wagon, giggle, sometimes even cuss. It's awful, Jim, and I don't know what to do about it, short of expelling the offenders. And if I did that, their parents would probably try to sue me."

"Well, Jerry, I've never been a father, but I'd be willing to talk to some of these kids. Mine being a new voice, they might listen. If you'll give me a name or two I can get started tomorrow morning."

Seventeen year old Charles Jensen walked into the church office at ten a.m. Pastor Whitworth introduced him to Jim, explaining that he is a traveling missionary whose interests lie in helping young people. Jensen's response:

"What's that got to do with me? I don't need no help."

"What about your addiction, Charles? Everybody knows about it; you can't be proud of that, can you?"

"That's my business, pastor, no body else's."

"But it IS my business, Charles. I'm the pastor of this church and it's my job to try to treat everyone the same. That's what Jesus would want, don't you agree?"

"Well, maybe, when you put it that way."

"Charles, I'm going to leave now but I want you to stay and talk to Mr. Dawson."

---

Before it was over, young Charles was in tears, telling Jim he'd do anything to kick the habit. He'd tried methadone, that didn't work. So what's left?.

Jim asked *why* the methadone treatments hadn't worked.

Charles admitted that he was usually stoned when he took methadone, and he probably didn't get the doses right; sometimes he'd skip a whole day.

"Okay, Charles. Here's what we're going to do. Beginning right now you and I are going to pray together. We're going to ask God to help you with your addiction. And you don't need me to pray. You can do it yourself, when you wake up in the morning and before you go to sleep at night. Your job is to skip the methadone and ask your mom to help you with a regular diet, three squares a day, no beer, no wine, zippo. I'm going to be here for another five days and before I hit the road again, I'll stop by and see how you're doing."

—————◆—————

Sixteen year old Cynthia Jameson appeared at the church office door and asked to see pastor Whitworth. When he answered he could see that she had been crying. Her makeup was smeared and between sobs she said she had a confession to make. He invited her in and asked her sit on the nearby sofa.

"What is it, Cynthia?"

"Pastor Whitworth, I really want to talk to your wife. It's a woman's thing, if you know what I mean."

"Sure, Cynthia, she's in the next room. I'll close the door and you won't be disturbed."

—————◆—————

Mrs. Whitworth, until last night I was a virgin. Then this boy—I won't use his name—and I had too much to drink. He's the captain of our football team and he thinks he can push other people around. Anyway, he told me he wanted to have sex, promised it wouldn't hurt, that I'd really like it. I'd never had sex before and I was curious to see what it was like. So we undressed and he got on top of me and pushed his penis inside me. And it hurt a lot, something broke and some blood came out. After we cleaned ourselves, he said he never wanted to see me again, that I was too young to be his girlfriend and he just stomped out and disappeared."

"Cynthia, that boy will do this again, to someone else. That's why you must give me his name. That way my husband can talk to his parents, tell them what happened. I'm certain they're both Christians, likely members of this church. Then it's up to them to see that this never happens again."

"Well, I guess you're right. His name is Bobby Lawson. He's seventeen and his parents *do* go to your church."

---

The Whitworths saw the issue as something that would probably damage the reputation of their church. They feared that as soon as the word got out about the Lawson boy and his treatment of Cynthia Jameson the local press would learn of it, probably leading to a neighborhood scandal. Even though their congregants were Christians, like most people they were prone to gossip. They decided to ask Jim Dawson to intervene. Jim has no official connection with the church, he's just passing through.

---

It took some doing, but Jim was able arrange a get-together with *both* Bobby Lawson and Cynthia Jameson.

"Okay, you two. We all know what happened and why you're here. I'm a stranger in these parts, I drive a truck for Wall Mart and I'm here for only a few days. But I do know something about adolescent behavior and you two have broken all the rules. Now, it seems to me that if we keep all this to just the three of us, the world need never know.

"Bobby, you could be accused of rape, even though—as I understand it—the sex was consensual. Cynthia, seems to me you used very poor judgment in agreeing to do what you did. So here's what we're going to do about this.

"The three of us are going to get down on our knees and pray to God that this never happens again and that no one needs to know about it. You two will say these prayers three times a day. I don't need to be here for that. And for the next few days, before I leave, the three of us will do the same, pray, pray, pray."

"Yes, Bobby, you wanted to say something?"

"I do. Cynthia and I *have* prayed about this. She has forgiven me and I have promised her that I will never say a word about this to anyone. We even laughed when we talked about this. We're going to be just pals, she and I, and we want our friends to see that.

"And, one last thing. We can never thank you enough. As a Christian, you have been a model for each of us. And we wish you safe travel, wherever you go."

# ELEVEN

ALTHOUGH HE DIDN'T LIKE IT, JIM DECIDED TO SPEND THE NIGHT in his rig's bunk bed. He could stretch out, the mini-mattress did it's job and when he awoke he felt refreshed and ready to go. His iPhone's map told him his next destination would be the Angola Travel Plaza, about ten miles from the center of Buffalo. Two hundred miles along I-90, about a four-hour run.

He opened his laptop, called up Wikipedia to see what it has to say about Buffalo, New York.

———◆———

'Buffalo is the second-largest city in the state of New York and the seat of Erie County. It lies at the eastern end of Lake Erie, adjacent to the Canadian border with Southern Ontario, and is at the head of the Niagara River. With a 2020 census population of 278,349, Buffalo is the 76th-largest city in the United States. The city and nearby Niagara Falls share the two-county Metropolitan Statistical Area. The MSA had an estimated population of 1.1 million in 2020, making it the 49th largest MSA in the United States. The Western New York region containing Buffalo is the largest population and economic center between Boston, Massachusetts and Cleveland, Ohio.

'Before French exploration, the region was inhabited by nomadic Paleo-Indians and, later, the Neutral, Erie and Iroquois nations. In the

18th century, Iroquois land surrounding Buffalo Creek was ceded through the Holland Land Purchase and a small village was established at its headwaters. Buffalo was selected as the terminus of the Erie Canal in 1825 after improving its harbor, which led to its incorporation in 1832. The canal stimulated its growth as the primary inland port between the Great Lakes and the Atlantic Ocean. Transshipment made Buffalo the world's largest grain port. After railroads superseded the canal's importance, the city became the largest railway hub after Chicago. Buffalo transitioned to manufacturing during the mid-19th century, later dominated by steel production. Deindustrialization and the opening of the St. Lawrence Seaway saw the city's economy decline, diversifying to service industries such as health care, retail, tourism, logistics, and education while retaining some manufacturing. The gross domestic product of the Buffalo–Niagara Falls MSA was $53 billion in 2019.

'During the early 19th century, Presbyterian missionaries tried to convert to Christianity the Seneca people on the Buffalo Creek Reservation. Initially resistant, some tribal members set aside their traditions and practices to form their own sect. Later, European immigrants added other faiths. Christianity is the predominant religion in Buffalo and Western New York. Catholicism has a significant presence in the region, with 161 parishes and more than 570,000 adherents in the Diocese of Buffalo. Major Protestant denominations in the area include Lutheran, Baptist, and Methodist. Pentecostals are also significant, and approximately 20,000 persons are non-denominational adherents.

'A Jewish community began to develop in the city with immigrants from the mid-1800s; about one thousand German and Lithuanian Jews settled in Buffalo before 1880. Buffalo's first synagogue, Temple Beth El, was established in 1847. The city's Temple Beth Zion is the region's largest synagogue.

'With changing demographics and an increased number of refugees from other areas on the city's East Side, Islam and Buddhism have expanded their presence. In this area, new residents have converted empty churches into mosques and temples. Hinduism maintains a small, active presence in the area, including the town of Amherst.

'A 2016 American Bible Society survey reported that Buffalo is the fifth-least "Bible-minded" city in the United States; only13 percent of its residents associate with the Bible.'

——————◆——————

'The village of Buffalo was named for Buffalo Creek. British military engineer John Montresor referred to "Buffalo Creek" in his 1764 journal, the earliest recorded appearance of the name. A road to Pennsylvania from Buffalo was built in 1802 for migrants traveling to the Connecticut Western Reserve in Ohio. Before an east-west turnpike across the state was completed, traveling from Albany to Buffalo would take a week; a trip from nearby Williamsville to Batavia could take more than three days.

'In 1813,British forces burned Buffalo and the northwestern village of Black Rock. The battle and subsequent fire was in response to the destruction of Niagara-on-the Lake by American forces and other skirmishes during the War of 1912. Rebuilding was swift, completed in 1815. As a remote outpost, village residents hoped that the proposed Erie Canal would bring prosperity to the area. To accomplish this, Buffalo's harbor was expanded with the help of Samuel Wilkeson. Itt was selected as the canal's terminus over the rival Black Rock. It opened in 1825, ushering in commerce, manufacturing and hydropower. By the following year, the 130-square-mile Buffalo Creek Reservation was transferred to Buffalo.

'Buffalo was incorporated as a city in 1832. During the 1830s, businessman Benjamin Rathbun significantly expanded its business district. The city doubled in size from 1845 to 1855. Almost two-thirds of the city's population was foreign-born, largely a mix of unskilled or poorly educated Irish and German Catholics.

'Fugitive slaves made their north to Buffalo during the 1840s. Buffalo was the terminus of the Underground Railroad, with many free blacks crossing the Niagara River to the Underground Railroad, with many free blacks crossing the Niagara River to Fort Erie, Ontario. During this time Buffalo's port continued to develop. Passenger and commercial traffic expanded, leading to the creation of feeder canals and rapid growth of the city's harbor.

'Unloading grain in Buffalo was a laborious job, and grain handlers working on lake freighters would make $1.50 a day in a six-day work week. Local inventor Joseph Dart and engineer Robert Dunbar built a grain elevator in 1843, adapting the steam-powered elevator. That elevator at first processed one thousand bushels per hour, speeding global distribution to consumers. Buffalo was the transshipment hub of the Great Lakes, and weather, maritime and political events in other Great Lakes cities had a direct impact on the city's economy. In addition to grain, Buffalo's primary imports included agricultural products from the Midwest—meat, whiskey, lumber and tobacco—and its exports included leather, ships, and iron products. The mid-19th century saw the rise of new manufacturing capabilities, particularly with iron.

'By the 1860s, many railroads terminated in Buffalo; they included the Buffalo, Bradford and Pittsburgh Railroad, the Buffalo and Erie Railroad, the New York Central Railroad and the Lehigh Valley Railroad. During this time, Buffalo controlled one-quarter of all shipping traffic on Lake Erie. After the Civil War, canal traffic began to drop as railroads expanded into Buffalo. Unionization began to take hold in the late 19th century, highlighted by railroad strikes in 1877 and 1892.'

'Buffalo has a humid continental climate, common in the Great Lakes region, and temperatures have been warming with the rest of the U.S. Lake-effect snow is characteristic of Buffalo winters with snow bands that produce intense snowfall in the city and surrounding area. However, Buffalo rarely gets the most snowfall in the state. The Blizzard of 1977 resulted from a combination of high winds and snow which accumulated on land and on the frozen Lake Erie. Although snow does not typically impair the city's operation, it can cause significant damage in autumn (as the October 2006 storm did. In November 2014, the region had a record-breaking storm which produced more than five and one-half feet of snow. Buffalo's lowest recorded temperature was –20 °F which occurred twice: on February 9, 1934, and February 2, 1961.

'Although the city's summers are drier and sunnier than other cities in the northeastern United States, its vegetation receives enough precipitation to remain hydrated. Buffalo summers are characterized by abundant sunshine, with moderate humidity and temperatures. The city benefits from cool humidity and temperatures from southwestern Lake Erie.'

---

Although Jim preferred the Covenant Church's worship format, he knew there were none of these in Buffalo and the nearest thing would be the Holy Trinity Lutheran Church, one of many churches together known as the Evangelical Lutheran Church in America, the ELCA. He opened his laptop and found the church's Web page: Reverend Franklin Jamison, parsonage address 2598 Senaca Avenue, hours 10 to 4 weekdays, closed Saturdays, Sunday worship services at eight, and eleven; phone 716 935 4002.

---

*The next morning, in Jamison's parsonage.*

"So, Mr. Dawson, you say you think of yourself as a traveling evangelist?"

"That's right, Pastor Jamison. I believe it's a mission the Lord wants me to pursue and, so far, I've been reasonably successful. This is my eleventh stop along Interstate 90, as it is said, 'so far, so good.'"

"Hmm. Well, I have a suggestion that just might challenge your record. You see, after the fall of Kabul to the Taliban a few weeks ago, my wife and I decided to offer our church facilities as a safe haven for those Afghans who've been able to leave. And the Lord has answered our prayers by bringing to us an Afghan couple, a man and his wife. His name is Faiz Akhtar and hers Maria. They have no children and the two of them are living in one or our small cottages, on the church's property."

"Language?"

"Yes. Faiz worked for the American embassy in Kabul. He learned to read and write English from a Christian missionary couple who lived there for eight years. They are members of our church and one of the last Americans to fly out of Kabul, before the Taliban took over. His spoken English is passable but he understands everything he hears."

"He's Muslim?"

"As he says, 'sort of.' He says he's not really a religious person but in Afghanistan one should at least pretend to be a Muslim."

"What does he think of Christianity?"

"We've not discussed that. If you want to talk to him you might bring that up."

---

Somewhat to his surprise, Jim quickly learned that Faiz Akhtar is an easygoing guy, apparently without pretense and with a hope that he'll be accepted by his new hosts. He readily admitted that he knows next to nothing about Christianity, in large part because back home in Afghanistan it was a subject no one dared talk about.

Jim made sure the man was comfortable and then asked Pastor Jamison's wife if she could bring them two cups of tea.

⸻

"Take your time drinking this, Faiz. What I have to say may take some time but I'm sure you'll find it interesting.

"I assume you're aware that your Quran was produced by Prophet Mohammad. He was born in or near Mecca about 600 a.d., that is six hundred years after the birth of Jesus Christ. By his account, he began receiving visions from the angle Gabriel when he was in his early twenties. These visions instructed him to write down stories that Gabriel would, over time, reveal to him. And we should recall that this angle Gabriel is the same angel who appeared to Mary with the incredible news that she would give birth to Jesus Christ.

"However, Mohammad had never learned to read or write and because he was illiterate, he shared these stories with friends. It was they who, many years later, composed what we now call the Quran, the holy book of Muslims.

"But, when one reads that book carefully, several questions arise. The Quran mentions what we Christians call the *Trinity,* the mysterious three persons of the Godhead: God, Jesus and the Holy Spirit. But the Quran describes the Trinity as consisting of God, Jesus and Mary, Jesus' mother. That's one indication that Mohammad had an imperfect understanding of Christianity.

"And there is more. A careful reading of the Quran reveals that Mohammad flatly denied the existence of the Trinity, insisting that

Allah was too majestic to have a son; he would have needed a wife, but Allah is all-powerful and all-seeing. He wouldn't need that kind of help.

"Further, the Quranic text acknowledges the historicity of a number of prophets, Abraham, Isaac, Jacob and Jesus. But it insists that there is no difference between these persons, thus denying the uniqueness of Jesus Christ.

"The Christian's fundamental understanding is that Jesus was crucified, dead, buried and that He rose again on the first Easter morning.

"But the Quran's text flatly denies His crucifixion, claiming that those who believe it are confused and wrong.

"And, perhaps the most compelling question is this: *Why would God change his mind after 600 years?* For us Christians, the answer can only be that He would not."

"Yes, I understand what you're saying, Mr. Dawson. And I have to admit that you make a compelling case. I'm going to share what you've said with my wife. With Pastor Jamison's help, and over time, it's possible that the two of us will become believers."

# TWELVE

KNOWING THAT SYRACUSE, NEW YORK WOULD BE HIS NEXT STOP, Jim pulled out his laptop and called up Wikipedia. This is what he found.

———◆———

'French missionaries were the first Europeans to come to this area, arriving to work with the Native Americans in the 1600s. At the invitation of the Onondaga Nation, one of the five nations of the Iroquois Confederacy, a group of Jesuit priests, soldiers set up a mission, known as Sainte Marie among the Iroquois, or Ste. Marie de Gannentaha, on the northeast shore of Onondaga Lake.

'Jesuit missionaries reported salty brine springs around the southern end of what they referred to as "Salt Lake", known today as Onondaga Lake in honor of the historic tribe. French fur traders established trade throughout the New York area among the Iroquois. Dutch and English colonists also were traders, and the English nominally claimed the area, from their upstate base at Albany, New York. During the American Revolutionary War the highly decentralized Iroquois divided into groups and bands that supported the British, and two tribes that supported the American-born rebels, or patriots.

'Settlers came into central and western New York from eastern parts of the state and New England after the American Revolutionary

War and various treaties with and land sales by Native American tribes. The subsequent designation of this area by the state of New York as the Onondaga Salt Springs Reservation provided the basis for commercial salt production. Such production took place from the late 1700s through the early 1900s. Brine from wells that tapped into salt beds in the Salina shale near Tully, New York, 15 miles south of the city, was developed in the 19$^{th}$ century. It is the north-flowing brine from Tully that is the source of salt for the "salty springs" found along the shoreline of Onondaga Lake. The rapid development of this industry in the 18$^{th}$ and 19$^{th}$ centuries led to the nicknaming of this area as "The Salt City".

'The original settlement of Syracuse was a conglomeration of several small towns and villages and was not recognized with a post office by the U.S. government. Establishing the post office was delayed because the settlement did not have a name. Joshua Forman wanted to name the village Corinth. When John Wilkinson applied for a post office in that name in 1820, it was denied because the same name was already in use in Saratoga County, New York. Having read a poetical description of Syracuse, Sicily, Wilkinson saw similarities to the lake and salt springs of this area, which had both "salt and freshwater mingling together". On February 4, 1820, Wilkinson proposed the name "Syracuse" to a group of fellow townsmen; it became the name of the village and the new post office.

'The first Solvay Process Company plant in the United States was erected on the southwestern shore of Onondaga Lake in 1884. The village was called Solvay to commemorate the inventor Ernest Solvay. In 1861, he developed the ammonia-soda process for the manufacture of soda ash (anhydrous sodium carbonate) from brine wells dug in the southern end of Tully valley, as a source of sodium chloride and limestone. The process was an improvement over the earlier Leblanc process. The Syracuse Solvay plant was the incubator for a large chemical-industry complex owned by Allied Signal in Syracuse. While this industry stimulated development and provided many jobs in Syracuse, it left Onondaga Lake as the most polluted in the nation.

'The salt industry declined after the Civil War, but a new manufacturing industry arose in its place. Throughout the late 1800s and early 1900s, numerous businesses and stores were established, including the Franklin Automobile Company, which produced the first air-cooled engine in the world; the Century Motor Vehicle Company; the Smith Corona company and the Craftsman Workshops, the center of Gustav Stickley's handmade furniture empire.

'On March 24, 1870, Syracuse University was founded. The State of New York granted the new university its own charter, independent of Genesee College, which had unsuccessfully tried to move to Syracuse the year before. The university was founded as coeducational. President Peck stated at the opening ceremonies, "The conditions of admission shall be equal to all persons... there shall be no invidious discrimination here against woman.... brains and heart shall have a fair chance. Syracuse implemented this policy and attracted a high proportion of women students. In the College of Liberal Arts, the ratio between male and female students during the 19th century was approximately even. The College of Fine Arts was predominantly female, and a low ratio of women enrolled in the College of Medicine and the College of Law.

'The first New York State Fair was held in Syracuse in 1841. Between 1842 and 1889, the Fair was held among 11 New York cities before finding a permanent home in Syracuse. It has been an annual event since then, except between 1942 and 1947, when the grounds were used as a military base during World War II and in 2020, due to the outbreak of the Covid 19 pandemic.

'As part of the racial incidents happening all over the country during the 1919 Red Summer, on July 31, 1919, there was a violent riot between white and black workers of the Syracuse Globe Malleable Iron Works.

'The manufacturing industry in Syracuse began to falter in the 1970s, as industry restructured nationwide. Many small businesses failed during this time, which contributed to the already increasing unemployment rate. Rockwell International moved its factory outside New York state. General Electric moved its television manufacturing operations to Suffolk, Virginia, and later offshore to Asia. The Carrier Corporation moved its headquarters out of Syracuse, relocated its manufacturing operations out-of-state, and outsourced some of its production to Asian facilities. Although the city population has declined since 1950, the Syracuse metropolitan area population has remained fairly stable, growing by 2.5 percent since 1970. While this growth rate is greater than much of Upstate New York, it is far below the national average during that period.'

Again, Jim wanted to connect with a local church and its pastor. His laptop showed several and he settled on the University United Methodist Church. He saw that the pastor is a woman, Marcia Owens. And more about her:

'Currently, Pastor Marcia serves the community on the board of the East Genesee Regent Association and board president at Welch Terrace, as a Tri Chair of the Central New York Poor Peoples' Campaign, through the ACTS Clergy Caucus and Upper New York for Full Inclusion group. She received her M.Div. from Boston University School of Theology, along with degrees from Onondaga Community College and SUNY Oswego in secondary education. She was a Pampered Chef consultant and is a certified life coach and spiritual coach. Pastor Marcia grew up north of Syracuse, where her parents still live. She is mom to AnnMarie, a 2020 graduate from Le Moyne College as an English major. She has one younger brother and is the best aunt to her niece and 2 nephews. Her cat, Oreo, still lives with her, attesting to her character as a human companion.'

———◆———

*In pastor Owen's study.*

"Thank you, pastor, for giving me some of your time. I know you're a busy person and I do appreciate it."

"Not a problem, Mr. Dawson. What can I do for you?"

"It's like this, pastor. I had breakfast this morning at one of your Applebee's restaurants. In the next booth I overheard a guy talking to a friend, and I could tell he's a Christian, said his name is William Brand- - -"

"Yes, a coincidence probably, but Bill Brand is a member of my church."

"Okay, then you probably know that he's a member of the local longshoreman's union"

"Yes, he's one of the local chapter's leaders; smart and determined."

"Well, what he told me may be news. He said at their last meeting the members agreed to go on strike. They believe that's the only way they can protest their limited wage-earning possibilities. He said the average longshoreman makes about $56,000 per year and they want the companies they work for to increase that to $60,000. That's not much of an increase, but it's the principle they're concerned about.

"Problem is, neither side is willing to budge. They've been arguing about this for more than a month and according to Mr. Brand neither side is willing to concede."

"Well, Mr. Dawson, you say you're a kind of traveling missionary, with deep pockets, any ideas?"

"Indeed. I've told Bill Brand that I'm giving him a draft for $4,000, that will cover the difference for one year. But I've also taken out a loan at my bank in Seattle—Seattle First National—with instructions that each year $4,000 be deposited to the longshoreman's account here in Syracuse for the next ten years.

"Again, as I say pastor, it's the answer to that question: 'What would Jesus do.'"

# THIRTEEN

Jim knew that Boston likely would be his last stop. He pulled out his laptop, hoping to find a rest area close to the city. Sure enough, the Metropolitan District Commission rest area was just what he wanted. It turned out to be a huge facility with plenty of room for his eighteen wheeler, toilet facilities, diesel and gasoline stations, a large Applebee's restaurant and small overnight units for those drivers who preferred avoiding expensive hotels.

Once parked and secure, Jim called up his favorite search engine—Wikipedia—and this is what he found.

——————◆——————

The city of Boston, Massachusetts is the capital and most populous city of the Commonwealth of Massachusetts and in the United States and 24th-most populous city in the country. The city covers 48.4 square miles.

Before European colonization, Boston was inhabited by the indigenous Massachusetts. There were small Native communities throughout what became Boston, who likely moved between winter homes inland along the Charles River where hunting was plentiful and summer homes along the coast where fishing and shellfish beds were plentiful. Through archeological excavations, one of the oldest Native fish weirs in New England was found on Boylston Street. Native people constructed it to trap fish several thousand years ago.

Boston's early European settlers first called the area Trimountaine, after three small mountains, only traces of which remain today. Later they renamed it *Boston* after the Boston in Lincolnshire, England, the origin of several prominent colonists. The renaming on September 7, 1763, was by Puritan colonists from England who had moved over from Charlestown earlier in their search for fresh water. Their settlement was at first limited to the Shawmut Peninsula, at that time surrounded by the Massachusetts Bay and Charles River and connected to the mainland by a narrow isthmus. The peninsula is thought to have been inhabited as early as 4000 BC.

In 1629, the region's first governor, John Winthrop, led the signing of the Cambridge Agreement, a key founding document of the city. Puritan ethics and their focus on education influenced its early history; America's first public school, Boston Latin School, was founded in Boston in 1635.

John Hull and the British schilling played a central role in the establishment of the Massachusetts Bay Colony and the Old South Church in the 1600s. In 1652 the Massachusetts legislature authorized John Hull to produce coinage. The Hull Mint produced several denominations of silver coinage, including the pine tree shilling, for over 30 years until the political and economic situation made operating the mint no longer practical.

Upon American independence from Great Britain, the city continued to be an important port and manufacturing hub as well as a center for education and culture.

King Charles II, for reasons which were mostly political, deemed the "Hull Mint" high treason, which had a punishment of being hanged, or drawn and quartered. On April 6, 1681, Edward Randolph petitioned the king, informing him the colony was still pressing their own coins which he saw as high treason and believed it was enough to void the charter. He asked that a writ of Quo warranto (a legal action requiring the defendant to show what authority they have for exercising some right, power, or franchise they claim to hold) be issued against the colony for the violations.

Boston was the largest town in the thirteen colonies until Philadelphia outgrew it in the mid-18th century. Boston's oceanfront location made it a lively port, and the city primarily engaged in shipping and fishing during its colonial days. However, Boston stagnated in the decades prior to the Revolution. By the mid-18th century, New York City and Philadelphia surpassed Boston in wealth. During this period, Boston encountered financial difficulties even as other cities in New England grew rapidly.

In 1773, a group of angered Bostonian citizens threw an East India Company shipment of tea into Boston Harbor as a response to the Tea Act, in an event known as the Boston Tea Party.

Many of the crucial events of the American Revolution occurred in or near Boston. Boston's penchant for mob action along with the colonists' growing lack of faith in either Britain or its Parliament fostered a revolutionary spirit in the city. When the British parliament passed the Stamp Act in 1765, a Boston mob ravaged the homes of Andrew Oliver, the official tasked with enforcing the Act, and Thomas Hutchinson, then the Lieutenant Governor of Massachusetts. The British sent two regiments to Boston in 1768 in an attempt to quell the angry colonists. This did not sit well with the colonists. In 1770, during the Boston Massacre, British troops shot into a crowd that had started to harass them. The colonists compelled the British to withdraw their troops. The event was widely publicized and fueled a revolutionary movement in America.

In 1773, Parliament passed the Tea Act. Many of the colonists saw the act as an attempt to force them to accept the taxes established by the Townshend Acts. The act gave birth to the Boston Tea Party, where a group of angered Bostonian citizens threw an entire shipment of tea sent by the East India Company into Boston Harbor. The Boston Tea Party was a key event leading up to the revolution, as the British government responded furiously with new laws, demanding compensation for the destroyed tea. This angered the colonists further and led to the American Revolutionary War. The war began in the area surrounding Boston with the battles of Lexington and Concord. Boston itself was besieged for almost a year during the siege of the city, which began on April 19, 1775. The New England militia impeded the movement of the British army. Sir William Howe, then the commander-in-chief of the British forces in North America, led the British army in the siege. On June 17, the British captured the Charlestown peninsula, during the battle of Bunker Hill. The British army outnumbered the militia stationed there, but it was a pyrrhic victory for the British because their army suffered irreplaceable casualties. It was also a testament to the skill and training of the militia, as their stubborn defense made it difficult for the British to capture Charlestown without suffering further irreplaceable casualties.

Several weeks later, George Washington took over the militia after the Continental Congress established the Continental Army to unify the revolutionary effort. Both sides faced difficulties and supply shortages in the siege, and the fighting was limited to small-scale raids and skirmishes. The narrow Boston Neck, which at that time was only about a hundred feet wide, impeded Washington's ability to invade Boston, and a long stalemate ensued. A young officer, Rufus Putnam came up with a plan to make portable fortifications out of wood that could be erected on the frozen ground under cover of darkness.

Putnam supervised this effort, which successfully installed both the fortifications and dozens of cannon on Dorchester Heights that Henry Knox had laboriously brought through the snow from Fort Ticonderoga. The astonished British awoke the next morning to see a large array of cannons bearing down on them. General Howe is believed to have said that the Americans had done more in one night than his army could have done in six months. The British Army attempted a cannon barrage for two hours, but their shot could not reach the colonists' cannons at such a height. The British gave up, boarded their ships and sailed away. Boston still celebrates "Evacuation Day" each year.

After the Revolution, Boston's long seafaring tradition helped make it one of the nation's busiest ports for both domestic and international trade. Boston's harbor activity was significantly curtailed by the Embargo Act—during the Napoleonic Wars—and the War of 1812. Foreign trade returned after these hostilities, but Boston's merchants had found alternatives for their capital investments in the interim. Manufacturing became an important component of the city's economy, and the city's industrial manufacturing overtook international trade in economic importance by the mid-19th century. A network of small rivers bordering the city and connecting it to the surrounding region facilitated shipment of goods and led to a proliferation of mills and factories. Later, a dense network of railroads furthered the region's industry and commerce.

During this period, Boston flourished culturally, as well, admired for its rarefied literary life and generous artistic patronage, with members of old Boston families—eventually dubbed the Boston Brahmins—coming to be regarded as the nation's social and cultural elites.

Boston was an early part of the Atlantic triangular slave trade in the New England colonies, but was soon overtaken by Salem, Massachusetts and Newport, Rhode Island. Boston eventually became a center of the abolitionist movement. The city reacted strongly to the Fugitive Slave Act of 1850, contributing to president Franklin Pierce's attempt to make an example of Boston after the Anthony Burns Fugitive Slave Case.

In 1822, the citizens of Boston voted to change the official name from the "Town of Boston" to the "City of Boston", and on March 19, 1822, the people of Boston accepted the charter incorporating the city. At the time Boston was chartered as a city, the population was about 46,226, while the area of the city was only 4.8 square miles.

In the 1820s, Boston's population grew rapidly, and the city's ethnic composition changed dramatically with the first wave of European immigrants. Irish immigrants dominated the first wave of newcomers during this period, especially following the area's great famine. By 1850, about 35,000 Irish lived in Boston. In the latter half of the 19th century, the city saw increasing numbers of Irish, Germans, Lebanese, Syrians, French Canadian and Russian and Polish Jews settling in the city. By the end of the 19th century, Boston's core neighborhoods had become enclaves of ethnically distinct immigrants with their residence yielding lasting cultural change. Italians became the largest inhabitants of the North End. Irish dominated South Boston and Charlestown and Russian Jews lived in the West End. Irish and Italian immigrants brought with them Roman Catholicism. Currently, Catholics make up Boston's largest religious community, and the Irish have played a major role in Boston politics since the early 20th century; prominent figures include the Kennedys, Tip O'Neil and John F. Fitzgerald.

Between 1631 and 1890, the city tripled its area through land reclamation be filling in marshes, mud flats, and gaps between wharves along the waterfront. The largest reclamation efforts took place during the 19th century; beginning in 1807, the crown of Beacon Hill was used to fill in a 50-acre mill pond that later became the Haymarket Square area. The present-day State House sits atop this lowered Beacon Hill.

Reclamation projects in the middle of the century created significant parts of the South End, West End, the Financial District and Chinatown.

Logan International Airport opened September 8, 1923. The Boston Bruins were founded in 1924 and played their first game at Boston Garden in November 1928.

Boston went into decline by the early to mid-20th century, as factories became old and obsolete and businesses moved out of the region for cheaper labor elsewhere. Boston responded by initiating various urban renewal projects, under the direction of the Boston Redevelopment Authority, established in 1957. In 1958, BRA initiated a project to improve the historic West End neighborhood. Extensive demolition was met with strong public opposition, and thousands of families were displaced.

The BRA continued to foster eminent domain projects, including the clearance of the vibrant Scollay Square area for construction of the modernist style Government Center. In 1965, the Columbia Point Health Center opened in the Dorchester neighborhood, the first Community Health Center in the United States. It mostly served the massive Columbia Point public housing complex adjoining it, which was built in 1953. The health center is still in operation and was rededicated in 1990 as the Geiger-Gibson Community Health Center. The Columbia Point complex itself was redeveloped and revitalized from 1984 to 1990 into a mixed-income residential development called Harbor Point Apartments.

By the 1970s, the city's economy had begun to recover after 30 years of economic downturn. A large number of high-rises were constructed in the Financial District and in the city's Back Bay. This boom continued into the mid-1980s and resumed after a few pauses. Hospitals such as Massachusetts General Hospital, Beth Israel Deaconess Medical Center and Woman's Hospital lead the nation in medical innovation and patient care. Schools such as the Boston Architectural College, Boston College, Boston University, the Harvard Medical School, Tufts University School of Medicine, Northeastern University, Massachusetts College of Art and Design, Tufts University, the Boston Conservatory and many others attract students to the area. Nevertheless, the city experienced conflict starting in 1974 over desegregation bussing, which resulted in unrest and violence throughout the public school system.

———————◆———————

Now it was time to locate a church and after a long look at his laptop he found what believed to be his best choice: The Church of the Covenant is a historic church at 67 Newbury Street in the Back Bay neighborhood of Boston, Massachusetts. A National Historic Landmark, it was built in 1865-1867 by the Central Congregational Church, and is now affiliated with the Presbyterian Church and the United Church of Christ. Its lead pastor is Rev Walter Brand, phone 617-385-2580, address 67 Newbury Street.

———————◆———————

*An hour later, in Reverend Brand's office*

"It's good of you to see me on such short notice, Reverend. My name is Jim Dawson and I drive an eighteen wheeler for Wall Mart. Back home near Seattle, I have quite a few friends who are Presbyterians, so I can relate to you and your congregation."

"Interesting, Mr. Dawson. What brings you here?"

"Well, I consider myself as a kind of traveling evangelist, a guy who tries to bring people to faith in Jesus Christ, whenever that opportunity presents itself."

"Not to change the subject, but how much do you know about Islam?"

"Quite a bit, as a matter of fact. I've done some research, have spoken about Islam. Why do you ask?"

"There's a woman in my congregation—her name is Donna Smith—who knows a lot about Islam. And she's very critical, not only of the Islamic faith but of anyone who claims to be Muslim. She talks to her church friends, hands out pamphlets, even has her own Web page. She uses that to criticize Islam, names a few people she knows to be Muslim and she doesn't seem to care who knows what's she's doing.

"But that came to a screeching halt about an hour ago when I got a phone call from a man who would identify himself only as 'Mustafa.' He told me that Ms Smith is now in 'their' custody. I had to conclude that she's been kidnapped by two or more Muslims - - -"

"Uh, you're certain about this?"

"More that certain, Mr. Dawson. Mustafa told me that Ms Smith will be released *only* when he and his friends receive a bank draft for one million dollars, with the payee line left blank. He said he would email me instructions for delivering the draft."

"Does the FBI know about this? Kidnapping is a federal crime, as you probably know."

"Yes, I've done that. I spoke with the Special Agent in Charge of the Boston Field Office and he said he'd assign one of his men immediately. His name is Roger White and I'm expecting him to show up within the hour.

"And, there's more. This Mustafa told me that he and his 'friends' have never forgotten what happened to Dzhokhar Tsarnaev and his brother Tamerlan. That's eight years ago, at the running of the Boston Marathon. The two brothers planted two homemade pressure cooker bombs which detonated near the finish line of the race, killing 3 people and injuring hundreds of others, including 17 who lost limbs."

"So this is a revenge thing, two crazy Muslims?"

"Exactly. And that's something Mr. White needs to know."

***

*Two house later in in Reverend Brand's office.*

"Mr. White, this is Jim Dawson. He's a Christian friend of mine who's staying here for a few days. He knows a lot about Islam and says he's willing to help."

"Good to meet you Mr. Dawson. You speak Arabic?"

"No, I'm afraid not. But I have an idea or two that might help in your investigation."

"Such as?"

"Let's say your Boston Field Office issues an APB. Every TV outlet and newspaper in the city picks up the story; and that story highlights the kidnappers' demand for the one million dollars ransom payment. And it reminds that the penalty for kidnapping, because it's a federal crime, can be up to 30 years in prison. Further, it says that if the kidnapper(s) will come forward and release their hostage, they might avoid a trial and incarceration."

"Where do you think this should happen?"

"That's not for me to decide. Reverend Brand?"

"Why not right here, in my church? It could be done quietly, no publicity."

"Agent White, what say you?"

"Good idea, let's do it."

***

At nine o'clock the next morning, 'Mustafa' arrives at Reverend Brand's church. Agent White and Jim Dawson are waiting. He tells the three that his real name is Khalil Muhammad Badawi and that he and three of his friends arranged the kidnapping. They live and work out of a run-down building near Boston's waterfront and report once a week to an ISIS facility in Damascus. Because they're short on funds they had hoped the ransom money would be cover their debts and future expenses. Now, however, those dreams are behind them.

Agent White tells them that he has received permission from FBI headquarters in Washington to allow the four of them to return to private life, *after* Donna Smith is returned, unharmed. They are to say nothing to anyone about what has happened. If they refuse, they'll go to trial and likely to prison.

At last report, Ms Smith is reunited with her church and family, the four Muslims have been ordered to return to Damascus.

Jim Dawson has decided that all's well that ends well in Boston. And he admits it, he's homesick. He's planning to return to the Pacific Northwest, via Interstate 90.

# FOURTEEN

JIM HAD PROMISED HIMSELF THAT ON HIS WAY BACK, HE'D STOP AT the same places as before. That meant finding pastor Marcia Owens in Syracuse. She had been gracious enough to find time for a long chat but what that chat revealed wasn't good news. The local longshoremen were on strike, demanding a four thousand dollar yearly pay increase. With pastor Owens' help, Jim had made a deal with the longshoremen's union, using his own financial reserves to meet the union's demand. Now it was time to see if his help had made a difference.

---

*In pastor Owens' office*

"It's great to see you again, pastor. But from the look on your face I'd say you're troubled about something."

"You're a mind-reader, Mr. Dawson. Yes, things are not as they should be. You may recall that several of the local longshoremen are members of my church. Ten days ago, one of these—one of our deacons, Robert Mayhew—told me that a friend of his was shot, not fatally, thank the Lord, but he's now in hospital."

"Why?

"The same as before, it's about wages and health benefits. The local union boss—Anthony Bianchi—is threating to order his men to stop working. If that were to happen the economy of this region would crash.

Some of my friends believe that Bianchi is part of an old Mafia gang and if that's true, his threat makes sense."

"Does the mayor know about this?"

"Yes, he does; and he's a member of my church."

"Okay, pastor, here's an idea. You tell the mayor what's going on. After he hears your suggestion, he'll call in Mr. Bianchi and tell him that if he persists he, the mayor, will revoke his license to operate. That is something even a former Mafia gang member can't ignore, else the whole city of Syracuse will demand he be tried in a court of law."

———◆———

And that is what happened. Three weeks later, the region's longshoremen were back at work, each of them trying forget what had nearly cost them their jobs.

# FIFTEEN

J IM'S NEXT LAYOVER WOULD BE IN BUFFALO AND HE WANTED TO check in with Reverend Franklin Jamison. He had fond memories of explaining the Gospel to Jamison's guest Faiz Akhtar, but while that was happening Faiz' wife Maria was in another room. Jim had to ask himself if Faiz had told his wife about their conversation and, if so, how did she respond? One way to find out, he'll ask her.

⋅⋅⋅⋅◆⋅⋅⋅⋅

After enjoying his second cup of tea with Reverend Jamison, Jim asked him if it were possible for him to spend a few minutes with Maria Akhtar.

Yes, she and her husband are living, temporarily, in one of the church's guest apartments.

⋅⋅⋅⋅◆⋅⋅⋅⋅

"Thanks for agreeing to see me, Maria. I'm curious about your experiences in Afghanistan. You should know that I'm a Christian, a faith that most folks in Afghanistan probably don't understand. Would I be right about that?"

"Up to a point, Mr. Dawson. When my husband and I were living in Afghanistan, I was not allowed to go to school. The Taliban were very strict about that. School was for boys and men only and the Taliban leaders claimed that their holy book, the Quran, said that women were only to help their husbands and, especially, to satisfy their sexual desires. There's a passage in the Quran they refer to. I have the text right here, translated into English:

> *A man marries to have an untroubled mind as far as housework is concerned—kitchen, cleaning, bedding. A man, supposing he is able to do without sex, is not capable of living at home alone. If he were to take on himself the task of doing all the housework, he would no longer be able to devote himself to intellectual work or knowledge. The virtuous wife, by making herself useful at home, is her husband's helpmate—and at the same time satisfies his sexual desires.*

"As you know, Mr. Dawson, my husband worked for your American embassy in Kabul, before the Taliban took over. I often went with him and the Americans were very patient with me while I struggled to learn your English language. That took nearly a year but then I was able to listen to your Voice of America broadcasts. That's how I learned about America and the Christian faith. I especially enjoyed listening to Franklin Graham, Charles Stanley and Chuck Swindoll. I learned how to pray and it wasn't long before I accepted Jesus as my Lord and Savior."

"That's beautiful, Maria. Do you know if there are other people from Afghanistan, living in this city?"

"Yes. There are about twenty of us and we help each other with household chores, baby sitting, shopping and other things. Why do you ask?"

"I'd want to get pastor Jamison's permission, but assuming he agrees, you and your husband could have your own ministry, right here in this church. You all speak the same language, and over time you could persuade your friends to accept Jesus."

"That could be expensive and we don't have much money."

"Not to worry, Maria. I can easily afford to cover any expenses that come your way."

---

Abdul Noor was the man who considered himself the leader of the small group of Afghan refugees in Buffalo. A construction engineer by trade, he had specialized in the building of one and two bedroom apartments in Kabul. But now, he was unemployed and even though he spoke reasonably good English, jobs were hard to find. He and his wife Asai were tiring of the free meals and quarters provided by pastor Jamison. The couple had stopped praying to Allah for help, believing that Muslim prayers coming out of Buffalo would do no good. And now this Maria woman was trying to get him and his wife to listen to her; something about Jesus.

---

"How much do you know about the Quran, Abdul?"

"Probably not as much as I should. In all my years in Kabul I never was able to read or write Arabic and that's the only language the mullahs would allow people to use."

"Okay, but you should know that the Quran was put together some 600 years *after* Jesus Christ's ministry here on earth. You may not be aware, but Muhammad himself did not write the Quran. He claimed he received visions from the angle Gabriel, the same angel to told Mary that she would bear a Son, Jesus. Because Muhammad was illiterate, he told these stories to his friends and they, eventually, put together what you now know as the Quran."

"Okay, so what?"

"Yes, but there's more that you should know. We Christians believe that Jesus was crucified, dead and buried; and on the third day He rose from the dead to take His place in heaven alongside His father God.

"But the Quran denies that Jesus was crucified; it claims that people who believe that are confused and wrong. It also claims that the Muslim's god Allah was too majestic to have had a son; he'd need a wife but all Allah has to say is 'be' and it is.

"And, frankly Abdul, we Christians find that impossible to believe. But the most important question we ask ourselves is this: Why would God change His mind after those six hundred years had passed? We believe that there's no reason why He would do that and that means we believe that Muhammad and his followers were wrong."

"So, you're saying the Quran is a fraud?"

"No, but what we *are* saying is that Muslims who believe in the Quran are mistaken, no more than that."

"Hmm. Well, I have to admit that you make a compelling case. I'm going to share with my wife what you've just told me and we'll sleep on it."

"Better still, Abdul, you and your wife should *pray* about it. I'm pretty sure if you do that you'll get an answer that will surprise you."

"Fair enough, Mr. Dawson. Let's have breakfast tomorrow morning before you leave Buffalo."

# SIXTEEN

B REAKFAST BROUGHT A WELCOME, IF NOT UNEXPECTED, SURPRISE. Over their final cup of coffee, Abdul told Jim that he and his wife *did* pray over the issue. And the message they received was clear: accept Jesus Christ as your Lord and Savior, and never look back.

---

Now, the return to Cleveland. Jim wanted to check in with pastor Jeremy Whitworth to learn if any progress had been made during his absence; progress with the young addicts who attended his church. He phoned the pastor, told him when he'd arrive. He drove his eighteen wheeler over the now-familiar route and arrived at the parsonage right on time.

---

"Good to see you again, Jim. I appreciate your calling first, that's given me some time to recall what's happened since you were last here and where we are today."

"Sort of a progress report?"

"Yes, and an encouraging one, too. You remember the Lawson and Jameson youngsters and their ill-advised sexual encounters. Well, each of those two has accepted Jesus as their Lord and Savior and it's no secret that you can claim some credit for what happened."

"Hmm, that *is* good news. Anything else?"

"Yes. Bobby and Cynthia have begun a ministry of their own, using this church as a meeting place. They invite their teen-age friends to come for coffee and conversation. The last time they did this there were at least ten of their friends, boys and girls. They sing hymns, the pray and they have promised each other to avoid sex until they marry. So, you might say it's one of those 'all's well that ends well' situations. And we, they, couldn't be happier. And they owe this mostly to you, Jim. You're doing good work and we want you to keep on with it."

# SEVENTEEN

J IM'S NEXT STOP WOULD BE IN CHICAGO. ON HIS PREVIOUS VISIT HE met Susan Dubois who—after several dates—thought she had fallen in love with him. She left him a note saying that she was returning to the Pacific Northwest and would try to forget about him.

"Well, that's probably for the best. She's a beautiful and talented woman but she's not the type I want to marry."

His reservation at the Palmer House/Hilton was in order and he checked into room1503, knowing he'd have a breath-taking view of Lake Michigan and its many cargo vessels.

Lying on the nightstand beside the bed he saw a note, hand written from a Mr. Roger Anderson, one of the hotel's assistant managers.

*Welcome to our hotel, Mr. Dawson. It's good of you to return. I have a matter I'd like to discuss with you, if you'd be willing to meet me in my office, ground floor Suite No 6.*

"Thank for agreeing to meet me on such short notice, Mr. Dawson."

"No problem, and you can call me Jim, most folks do."

"Good. You see, Jim, I know from your previous visit here that you are a Christian, as am I. It's our hotel's policy to welcome all guests, no matter their color, sex or religious affiliation. And that's where the problem lies- - -"

"How so?"

"Because we know that a few of our guests are members of what's left of the Mafia, here in Chicago. We send copies of our guests' registration cards to the FBI's Chicago field office and their records tell us that there are two former Mafia men—Luigi Columbo and Romano Russo—staying here, in one of our more expensive suites, number 1050 on the tenth floor.

"But, there's more. With my permission, the FBI has wired that tenth floor suite. One of their Special Agents—Charles Polk—has been listening to their conversations for the past two days. They talk about a 'shakedown operation' (their words) which involves the mayor's office. One of his staff members is accepting bribe money to keep silent about the Mafia's presence here in Chicago."

"That sounds like an indictable crime."

"Yes, it is. But FBI headquarters in Washington wants to wait a few more days to see if more evidence becomes available."

---

*Four floors below, in room 631, Columbo and Russo are arguing about something.*

"Luigi, I told you not to trust that woman. She's nothing but poison."

"Maybe so, Romano, but she's the key to this operation. She knows everyone on the mayor's staff and the info she gives us is always spot on."

"Well, I still don't like it. Suppose she rats on our operation, tells the cops or the FBI? Then where are we?"

"Hey, remember our deal with her. As long as she does what she's doing, she'll eventually get close to ten thousand bucks, right out of our treasury."

---

*Loose lips sink ships. What the two man don't know is that Special Agent Charles Polk is listening to—and recording—every word. And he believes that now, with this recording, he can seek an indictment from one of the local judges. But Jim Dawson has another idea.*

---

"Charles, these two guys only four floors below. With your permission, I'd like to hustle down there and talk to them."

"Talk about what?"

"I want to tell them that the jig's up. That you and your colleagues know all about their plan. I'll offer them 50 thousand dollars, if they'll agree to talk to you, tell you everything they know about their activities. I can afford the fifty thousand, whether or not it actually gets into their hands is another matter."

---

*Jim knocks on the door and two surprised men open it. He introduces himself.*

"Hi, sorry to interrupt, but I need to talk to you two. I'm Jim Dawson and I've been upstairs with a couple of FBI agents. They've bugged your room and have been listening to your conversations for the past thirty minutes or so."

"What the hell?!"

'Yes, it's true. Let me come in and I'll explain everything."

"Okay, but it better be good!"

"Look, I'm a private citizen. I don't work for the government but I do have a couple of friends in the FBI. And they've given me permission to make you two an offer."

"Such as?"

"You need to understand that my FBI friends know all about your dealings with the mayor's office. They have enough evidence to arrest the two of you. As you know, Chicago is not very happy with the Mafia; too many robberies and killings. If you were to go to trial you could easily wind up in prison, maybe as many as twenty years."

"So? Get to the point. Where are you going with this?"

"Okay. You sit down with my FBI friends and you identify each of your Mafia buddies: names, addresses, phone numbers, everything. They'll go to their computers to make sure you've told the truth. And, assuming you have, they'll offer you what we call the witness protection program. Maybe you're heard of it."

"Maybe so, maybe no. Tell us more."

"Sure. They'll give you new names, new drivers licenses, ID cards, the works. Any name you want. You'll probably want to leave Chicago, go somewhere where nobody knows you. They'll pay for that, too. You'll be in a kind of probation status, meaning that every six months or so an FBI agent will make sure you're behaving yourselves, going to work every day, raising a family if you want to do that."

"And what if we refuse?"

"Hard to say, but I'd count on at least twenty years in a federal prison."

———— ⋯⋯◆⋯⋯ ————

*As in all federal witness protection programs, the names and locations of those using the program are never revealed. But it can be assumed that Luigi Columbo and Romano Russo are somewhere in the United States, earning, one would hope, an honest living.*

# EIGHTEEN

HｴｴH

After a good night's sleep, Jim climbed aboard his eighteen-wheeler and set out for Madison. He had fond memories of his earlier visit with Doctor Smithson and it would be good to see the man again. As he thought about it the good doctor had a tough job, trying to enforce the protocols for Wisconsin's dairy industry. Absent those rules, consumers could only guess at whether their milk was safe to drink; a particularly worrisome thing for young mothers with infants to feed.

⸺◆⸺

"It's good to see you again, Jim, and I appreciate your taking the time to stop by."

"Not a problem, Doctor, it's good to be here. How are things going?"

"Not as well as I'd like, to be honest about it."

"Trouble?"

"I'm afraid so. You'll recall that we were having trouble with the local union chapter of the AFL/CIO. Well, that problem hasn't gone away. One of its members, Leonardo Abdo, is a convicted drug addict. After two years in jail, he's now out on probation, has to meet his probation officer at least once a month."

"What's the problem?"

"Mr. Abdo has persuaded several of our dairy farmers to cheat on the pasteurization process; they don't heat the milk enough to kill the latent bacteria. By doing this they save, maybe, a penny or two per gallon of milk, but with the volume they're dealing with, it adds up to enough money to make it worthwhile."

"Can you prove this?"

"Certainly. several cases of salmonella poisoning in children have shown up. The parents are furious and frightened, and I understand they're about to sue Mr. Abdo, or even the union's local chapter."

"Any fatalities?"

"Thank the good Lord, not yet."

"How many people know about this?

"So far, only those of us who are involved. We don't want to create a panic among the population, that wouldn't help either side of the dispute."

"What if I were to talk to this Mr. Abdo? I might be able to help."

"His phone number is in the local directory."

———◆———

*It was a tense meeting. Jim chose to invite Mr. Abdo to one of the city's Italian restaurants. Over pizza and beer, he told Abdo that he was aware of the man's crimes—threatening the health of the city's children—and if he failed to stop it Jim would see to it that his probation officer was notified and that would mean a return to prison.*

*Abdo saw no way out and decided to give it up. At last report, each of the infected children has recovered and returned to their families. Abdo is back in prison where he will serve out his term.*

# NINETEEN

Jim's next stopover would be at Sioux Falls. He was anxious to connect with city councilman Dan Thomas and learn more about the mayor's plans for taxing the city's businesses. Before leaving Madison he left a call with Thomas, telling him he'd be there for two days.

---

*In Thomas's office.*

"So, Jim, you look none the worse for wear, considering all the driving you've been doing."

"Thanks for that, Tom. Yeah, I've been on the road long enough to know how to take care of myself. Plenty of sleep, drink lots of water, three squares a day, no tobacco. Once you get used to the routine, it's pretty easy.

"How are things going for you?"

"Not as well as I would like. Since you were last here, I've learned a few things about our mayor, Richard Arnold. For one, the man is a multi-millionaire. He inherited close to five million dollars from his grandfather and he's using some of that money to buy votes."

"No kidding! Can you prove it?"

"Sure. People talk and I know at least three friends who would gladly testify in court, if it comes to that."

"Do you know how he's doing this? He must have help."

"He does. Any politician, like Arnold, has a lot of friends, folks who have contributed money to his campaigns. He has persuaded some of them—I don't know for sure how many—to infiltrate (his word) as many churches as possible, try to persuade church members to gin up a petition. That petition would demand that his proposed tax on the John Morell meat packing plant be kept on the ballot. It's crazy, Jim. That business provides more employment and income for this region than any other."

· · · · · · ◆ · · · · ·

Richard ('Dick' to his many friends) Arnold considered himself the most important and successful politician in all of South Dakota. He had been on the university's debate team, took a degree in law from the same university, married one of the school's most beautiful women and when his grandfather died, he became one of the richest men in the region.

His first experience with buying votes came when he was a candidate for editing the law school's newsletter, *Law in South Dakota.* That decision was in the hands of five faculty members and each of them found an envelope containing one thousand dollars, delivered through the school's internal mail system. The source of these funds was never identified but there was no doubt that it was Richard Arnold.

Now, as mayor of Sioux Falls, he was accepting 'insurance' payments from the city's major businesses. The payments were calculated at five percent of each company's gross annual income. Make the payments or have your business license revoked.

· · · · · · ◆ · · · · ·

"Okay, Dan, now that we know all this, what do you think we should do about it?"

"Easy, Jim. We ask him to come to my office and we confront him with what we know. He won't like it but when he hears our plan, he'll give it up."

"The plan?"

"Yes. I've already drafted the scripts. One each for our two newspapers and four for our television stations. I've contacted the manager of KCSD, the PBS outlet for this region; also, KKTW for Fox network outlet.

---

When confronted with 'the plan,' mayor Richard Arnold told his hosts that he would submit his resignation the next morning and he expected it to be accepted by the city council. All this on condition that none of his misdeeds be made public.

# TWENTY

KNOWING HIS NEXT STOP WOULD BE RAPID CITY, SOUTH DAKOTA, Jim sent an email to pastor Wayne Hansen, asking him if it would be okay if the two could get together again for a brief visit.

---◆---

*The next day, in Hansen's office*

"It's good to see you again, Jim. How's the job?"

"Couldn't be better, pastor. But I wanted to drop by to catch up on your dealings with you wayward teenagers. As I recall, one of them—Nancy Gardner—feared she was pregnant. How did that story end?"

"Yes, Jim. That may be the best-kept secret in this city. Nancy had an abortion and only a few of us know about it. As an immature Christian, she was especially troubled, knowing what Jesus had to say about the sanctity of marriage."

"What about the boy, Billy Norris?"

"When Billy's parents learned what had happened they insisted that he go to the girl's parents and apologize. He did that and now Billy and Nancy are dating, telling others they're just good friends.

"And, best of all, the two of them are attending my Young Life meetings. They were reluctant at first but now, with the others, the pray and sing together and partake in the Lord's Supper once each month.

It's something like a blooming love story. One of the local newspapers has sent a reporter to write an article about it."

"Do you think the two would be willing to go on television? Tell their story to thousands?"

"Why don't you ask them? They're in the next room practicing for next Sunday's service."

———————◆———————

What happened next, some said, was a God-given miracle. Withing six weeks' time Young Life groups had self-organized throughout the state. Billy and Nancy—with the help of two professionals and Jim Dawson's money—developed their own television show; a half-hour spot appearing every Sunday morning at nine. Its theme: teenagers throughout the state are encouraged to think about what the Bible has to say about premarital sex; AVOID it. Talk to your parents and your pastors. Take pride in celibacy, save yourself for marriage.

One of the television producers thought it a good idea to have Jim Dawson appear on the show, he being the one responsible for what was happening. But Jim declined, insisting he was only doing God's work and the results of those efforts could speak for themselves.

And it was time to move on. He could leave Rapid City, knowing that he had done as much as he could.

———————◆———————

His next stop would be Gillette, Wyoming and he was curious to learn what happened to the people involved in that guided missile program. It wouldn't take long to find out, Gillette was barely a two-hour drive from Rapid City.

But Jim was tired and he remembered his last visit. He pulled his eighteen wheeler into the Flying J tarmac, asked for permission to leave it there overnight. Then, as before, he took a cab to the Radisson Hotel and a good night's sleep.

⸺✦⸺

The next morning, after breakfast, Jim asks the hotel's concierge if it's possible to put a phone call through to Gillette's National Guard captain, Jack Nelson. After getting the number, Jim steps into a phone booth and places his call.

"Captain Nelson? Yes, this is Jim Dawson, you might remember me from the last time I was here. If it's not too much trouble, Sir, I'd like to meet with you; I have something to share but it should be done face-to-face. I'm calling from the Radisson Hotel and I can wait for you here."

⸺✦⸺

A momentous meeting. Jim tells the captain of his earlier conversation with the American G.I. who served in Iraq, Billy McKay. McKay told Jim of an on-going plot to sabotage the High Mobility Artillery Rocket system, make it inoperable so that Army will scrap it. But it hasn't happened yet and if you act quickly you can apprehend the guy before he has time to succeed.

⸺✦⸺

The 'guy' is slightly-retarded 22 year old corporal David Short, a high school dropout who fancies himself as an electronics specialist, but only because he knows how to use his iPhone. In the ensuing investigation it was impossible to learn how he got his hands on the plans but when confronted by the authorities he quickly admitted to what he was trying to do.

And so the High Mobility Artillery Rocket system remains in place and ready to be used whenever needed.

# TWENTY ONE

J IM KNEW THAT THE NEXT LEG OF HIS JOURNEY, FROM GILLETTE, Wyoming to Billings, Montana, would take about five hours, given the mountainous terrain to be covered. He recalled his previous visit, a dustup in a parking lot, involving the attempted rape of a young Christian woman.

He had the name and cell number of one of the police officers and decided that, once he got there, he'd give him a call.

---

"Sergeant Jacobs, here. How many I help you?"

"Sergeant, this is Jim Dawson. You may remember me from my last visit. We were in a parking lot and you spoke to a Donna Waite who had moments earlier freed herself from an attempted rape. Whatever happened?"

"Yes, I do remember that. His name was John Valko and there was a year-old outstanding warrant for his arrest for attempted rape. Come to think of it, he's been in trouble again, this time for attempting to rob a Seven Eleven store at that rest area alongside Interstate 90."

"Is that all?"

"No, it's not. As we speak, Mr. Valko is in the Yellowstone County jail, awaiting trial for robbery. His attorney is planning to enter a plea bargain: a fifty thousand dollar donation to the city's public library in exchange for his freedom. But those in the know say it will never happen."

"So, if he's convicted, what then?"

"Likely ten to fifteen hears in jail."

"Sergeant, could you do me a huge favor?"

"Sure, why not?"

"Okay, you find Donna Waite and tell her that Mr. Valko will never hurt anyone again. And please add that her friend Jim Dawson said so."

———◆———

Jim looked at his watch and decided to push on. Missoula was five hours away but he was pretty sure he could get there before dark. And he did, stopping only once to refill the vehicle's diesel tanks. There was a Motel Six at the edge of town and he decided to spend the night there, only sixty dollars, buffet breakfast included.

The next morning Jim found the phone number he was looking for, the Missoula Manor where his Vietnam Vet friend Sam Dawkins should be living. He dialed the number and the receptionist told him that Mr. Dawkins is still here and he should be glad to see you.

"Tell him, please, that I'll be there in about ten minutes."

———◆———

It was an emotional occasion, old Sam had tears in his eyes, seeing his sole benefactor for the first time in too many months. They were sitting across from each other in the Manor's downstairs recreation room.

"So, how are you my friend? You're looking well."

"Jim, I gotta tell you. This place is perfect. The food is good and the managers treat all of us as though we're some kind of royalty. But there's something you need to know about, that the others here don't."

"Sure, Sam, what is it?"

"I have a friend who's living in one of the city's homeless shelters. His name is Abdul Shakor. He's an Afghan refugee who used to work as a translator in our American embassy in Kabul, before the Taliban took over. He's a very bright guy. He speaks native Pashto and he learned to speak English while he was there, but now he says he can't find work."

"Could I meet this friend of yours?"

"Not a problem, I know how to find him. If you'll call a cab we can be there in ten minutes."

———◆———

Their meeting went on for nearly an hour but when it was over Jim's plan was put in motion. Abdul Shakor will fly from Missoula to Seattle where he'll be met by a representative of an organization that calls itself The Christian Coalition, a group of Christian representatives from the region's churches. The organization has a 501 (c) 3 designation with the IRS which means that donations to the group are tax-free. As soon as he arrives in Seattle, Abdul will be taken to the Common Broadway apartment complex which he will call home for the first sixty days. When he is settled, Abdul will become a key participant in CC's Afghan refugee program, finding housing and employment for the adults and schooling for the children. All of this to be financed by Jim Dawson.

# TWENTY TWO

H E HAD TO ADMIT IT. JIM DAWSON WAS HOMESICK. HE'D BEEN ON the road far too long. Time to return to his roots, maybe even sell his eighteen wheeler which had been his home, all those days and nights.

Rather than stopping in Spokane, he decided to push on, all the way to Mercer Island. When he finally arrived, it was dark and he pulled into the island's park and ride, just off Interstate 90. He crawled into his bunkbed and slept until eight the next morning. From there he drove his eighteen wheeler to the Peterbilt lot, found its owner and told him he was through with the vehicle. Maybe it could be resold as used, but it didn't matter.

He hailed a cab and asked to be driven to Mercer Island. While waiting for the cab he called pastor Jeremy Lewis and told him he was back and could they meet first thing tomorrow morning?

*In pastor Lewis' office.*

"You look tired, Jim. And it's no wonder, after all those miles on the interstate. But I have to tell you, I've received at least a dozen phone calls from those pastors that you've befriended along the way, each one of them marveling at your ability to spread the Gospel."

"Yeah, thanks for that, pastor. In a way the Gospel sells itself if people will only listen and think about it. But now that I'm home I need to take some time off, rest up a bit and get on with my life."